The Cats that Flooded the Manor

Karen Anne Golden

Copyright

This book or eBook is a work of fiction.

Names, characters, places and incidents are products of my imagination or are used fictitiously. Nyack and Manhattan, New York, are real places. So are Louisville, Kentucky, and Scottsburg, Indiana. The towns of Erie, Seagull and Melody, Indiana, are not.

The characters I create do not exist, nor have they ever lived in these cities.

Any resemblance to actual events, locales, persons or cats, living or dead, is entirely coincidental.

Edited by Vicki Braun

Book cover concept by Karen Anne Golden

Graphic design by Rob Williams

Copyright © 2022 Karen Anne Golden

All rights reserved.

ISBN: 9798434622714

Table of Contents

Chapter One 1
Chapter Two 19
Chapter Three 27
Chapter Four 34
Chapter Five...50
Chapter Six 65
Chapter Seven 75
Chapter Eight 82
Chapter Nine 97
Chapter Ten 102
Chapter Eleven..113
Chapter Twelve..128
Chapter Thirteen 149
Chapter Fourteen 158
Chapter Fifteen 170
Chapter Sixteen...192
Chapter Seventeen 215
Chapter Eighteen 226
Chapter Nineteen 232

"Sometimes when folks follow Cupid's arrow, it doesn't lead them where they want to go."

Chief Merrill, Chief of Police, Melody, Indiana

Chapter One

Erie, Indiana
Mid-October, 2018
Monday

Katherine "Katz" Cokenberger, a thirty-one-year-old computer professional and heiress to millions of dollars, sat on a wingback chair in the living room of her pink Victorian mansion. The torn lining at the bottom of the chair was where two of her cats hid their stolen loot, but not all of her felines were thieves.

Katherine was owned by seven cats that were extraordinary in many ways. Each feline had a unique ability beyond the realm of the everyday house cat. Scout and Abra, seal-point Siamese littermates, were part of a magician's act until they were retired as popular performers. They staged a macabre death dance when a crime was going to be committed, or had already taken place.

Iris, another seal-point, was bought at a swanky cattery in Manhattan, New York. She was a kleptomaniac and several times had stolen items that were key evidence toward solving crimes. Lilac, a lilac-point Siamese, was a gift from Katz's ex-fiancé, who was the first to meet an untimely death at the pink mansion. Lilac was often seen at Katherine's computer, where Internet searches provided additional clues to unraveling a mystery, but no one knew for sure if she was the one who surfed the Web, or if it was another cat.

Abby, a golden-eyed Abyssinian, was the reason why Katherine moved from Manhattan to the small town of Erie. Katherine's great aunt's will provided that if she moved to Indiana, lived in her seventeen-room mansion, and took care of her cat, she'd inherit millions. It was easy for her to accept the terms. She'd been fired from her job (the boss called it downsizing), she was looking for a change, and she fell in love with Abby, who was a very sweet, affectionate cat. Abby's special gift was stealing evidence from criminals, hiding it in the wingback chair, and later dropping it near an investigator's foot. Abby was perfect in many ways, except for one character flaw; she ate holes in wool sweaters.

The latest additions to the feline family were two rowdy seal-point boys, named Dewey and Crowie. They belonged to a former student who could no longer take care of them. The two Siamese hadn't developed their exclusive trait, but Katherine believed they would in the future.

Katherine married Jake, a history professor who taught at a nearby university. She was selective about her friends and counted the number of close friends on one hand. Her friend Colleen was her best friend. They'd grown up in Brooklyn, went to the same school and graduated together. While Katherine was an only child, Colleen lived next door with her mother and four brothers.

Colleen's mother Maggie, affectionately called Mum, was a single mom working a nine-to-five job and raising five children. Mum called Katherine her daughter, yet Katherine didn't think of Mum as her mother. In the past, whenever Mum came into town, there was bound to be some kind of drama, mostly just annoying incidents, but one time she let in a murderer who shot Jake. The bullet nearly killed him. This was the main reason why Katherine didn't trust Mum, and Jake positively disliked her.

When Katherine moved to Erie, Colleen soon followed, and attended the same university where Jake taught. Colleen recently married Jake's cousin, Daryl, who was a deputy sheriff in the neighboring county.

Over time, the pink mansion had acquired the unsavory name of "murder magnet" because of the number of crimes that had been committed there. Stevie Sanders, a handsome neighbor and ex-con, still pined for the woman he loved. She was the key witness to bringing down a New Jersey crime organization. Rachael was whisked away from Erie to enter the Witness Protection Program; her whereabouts were unknown. Stevie's daughter, Salina, was a senior in high school and regarded Katherine as her best friend and mother figure. Her mom had died of a drug overdose years before. Stevie and Salina still lived in the American Foursquare house next door to the pink mansion.

It was the sound of Katherine's cellphone's ringtone that snapped her out of her daydream. She rose from her chair and looked for her phone, then realized she'd forgotten where she'd put it. The simple action woke up the cats that had been lounging in various cozy beds in the spacious living room. "Where's my phone?" she asked out loud.

Iris, who saw her opportunity to reclaim the wingback chair, slinked out from behind it, but was too late. Three streaks of fur, belonging to Abby, Lilac and Crowie, quickly darted to it and sat down with their front paws tucked under them. Iris preferred the company of Dewey, so she sounded a loud "yowl" of disapproval and trotted off to find the Siamese.

The phone rang again.

"Dang! Where is it?"

"Waugh," Scout cried, vacating the cozy bed she shared with Abra, who was too sleepy to wake up. She moved to the Eastlake marble-top cabinet and jumped up. She stretched her long, lithe body into an ancient Egyptian Bastet pose and patted the phone.

"Smart girl," Katherine praised, petting Scout on the head. She picked up the phone and read the familiar name on its screen. "Hey, Colleen, how are you?" she answered.

"Katz, I'm just outside of Erie. Can I come over? I need to talk to you," Colleen said in a worried voice.

"Yes, of course. What's wrong?"

"Oh, it's a long story. I'll tell you when I get there." Colleen hung up without saying goodbye.

Katherine turned from the cabinet and began a customary head count of the cats' locations. Abby, Lilac and Crowie were still on the wingback chair, now curled up in one breathing fur ball. Iris had joined Dewey in his cozy bed by the turret window and was washing his ears. Abra was still in her cozy bed and snoring.

"Okay, treasures of mine, Colleen is coming over. She seems upset. I want you to be on your best behavior." Katherine spoke to her cats often because she believed they understood her.

She walked to the door and looked out one of the sidelights. Colleen had just arrived and was getting out of her car. She walked briskly to the mansion with her long, red hair flying.

Katherine opened the door. "Come in. What on earth is wrong?"

Colleen caught her breath and said, "Mum has gone missing."

"Come in and sit down. What's going on?"

Four of the cats, sensing stressful news, scattered to different parts of the mansion, except for Iris, who reclaimed her chair, and Scout and Abra, who were standing nearby with their ears perked to attention.

Colleen dropped into the wingback next to Iris's chair. "Let me start from the beginning. Mum met this guy on the Internet in one of those online dating sites. They emailed back and forth over the past few weeks, then he asked her to fly out to meet him."

Katherine looked shocked. "I thought Mum had sworn off of men? Why couldn't this man fly to Manhattan to meet her?"

Colleen shook her head. "I don't have a clue."

"Where does this guy live?"

"In southern Indiana in a place called Melody."

"Never heard of it."

"I Googled it. It's located on the banks of the Ohio River with a population of about six thousand people. The closest airport is in Louisville, Kentucky, which is about an hour drive from Melody."

"So, do you think you can talk her out of it?"

"Fat chance."

"Why? Surely, Mum isn't going to fly out to meet this guy?"

Colleen clucked her tongue with a disapproving "tsk." "Going to? She flew out from LaGuardia last Friday and I haven't heard from her since."

"She's not answering your texts?"

"Nadda. Texts, emails or phone calls. She's not responding. I'm worried sick that something terrible has happened to her. I can only imagine."

"It's only Monday. She's been gone just a few days. Maybe she's really having a good time and doesn't want to spoil it by—"

Colleen interrupted, "Hearing from a worried daughter trying to find out if she's okay and hasn't become the victim of an ax murderer."

"I wouldn't go that far. It could be as simple as her phone needs to be charged, or she lost it."

"Mum's pretty good with recharging her phone. I've told her that if she loses her phone, she can walk in practically any store and buy a burner phone."

"Out of curiosity, do you normally text Mum every day?"

"Yes, ever since she fell off the wagon and was boozing it up again, I check on her every day. She promised to text me as soon as her plane landed in Louisville. It's unlike her to go stone silent."

"Have you asked Daryl to check law enforcement databases to find out about this guy? At least, to see if he has a criminal record."

"I have his name, but I'm sure it's fake."

"Fake?"

"John Smith. There must be gazillion John Smiths in the world."

"Did you do a search of Melody's phone numbers?"

"I could only find two landline numbers for men named John Smith. I called both of them. Not one of them knew anything about a date with a sixty-year-old Irish woman. If there are more John Smiths in Melody and they have cellphones, I wouldn't know how to get those numbers."

"True, but Colleen, what are you going to do?"

"That's where you come in. I was going to ask you to go to Melody with me and help me track down Mum."

"Me? You want me to come?"

"Yes. I can't very well go on my own."

"You could, but I know you don't like to go places on your own. When would you want to go?"

"As soon as possible."

"There's no way I can leave today. I'm teaching a word processing class this afternoon and I have a committee meeting tomorrow," Katherine said, listing her scheduled appointments. "And, I can't leave Scout and

Abra behind for long periods of time because they'll drive Jake nuts with their 24/7 howling until I get back."

"I know all about their separation anxiety, so that's why I'm looking for a place that allows pets. Did you know there are no motels in Melody?" Colleen asked rhetorically. "The closest chain motels are by the interstate where you exit the highway to Melody, just south of Scottsburg."

"Oh, I know where that is. Did you find one that allows pets?"

"Yes, one, but it's booked. As a matter-of-fact, all three of the motels are booked. Besides, Katz, it's like an hour away from where we want to be. However, all is not lost. I looked at my trip advisor app and Melody has several bed and breakfasts."

Katherine observed, "Okay, I'm fine with a B&B as long as I can take Scout and Abra."

"Waugh," Scout agreed. Abra was too busy scratching her chin to answer.

"I called every single one of them and they're booked, except for one."

"Booked? Why? What's the attraction?"

"Melody is listed on the Register of Historic Places. Katz, it sounds like it's right up your alley because it's full of mom-and-pop restaurants and shops, and . . . Colleen paused for emphasis, then finished, "tons of antique stores."

"Erie's on the Register. We have everything you mentioned, but only one B&B. The owner is always complaining about lack of business. Why is Melody so popular?"

"Katz, it's the height of the leaf season. People drive from miles around to see Indiana's autumn leaves. Fall festivals are taking place everywhere."

"Yes, this is true. Jake and I went to the covered bridge festival last weekend. Melody does sound like my kind of place."

"I found an Airbnb walking distance to downtown."

"What's that?"

"Airbnb is short for air bed & breakfast. These places are popping up all over the country. People can rent their homes or condos to guests who book online."

"I don't get it. What's the difference between the two?"

"A B&B is what it is. A room for the night and a breakfast. The owner lives in or near the building. However, an Airbnb is the entire place and the owner doesn't live there."

"I like that idea. Does the Airbnb allow cats?"

"This morning, I spoke to the owner of one and she allows pets. She said cats were allowed, but they have to be confined to the guest's room."

Katherine chuckled. "As if I'd let my cats run amok in a place they didn't know. What's the name of this place?"

"It's called Melody Manor," Colleen answered, then frowned. "I have a gut feeling something is wrong, terribly wrong."

"Wrong with the Airbnb?" Katherine scrunched up her face in confusion. "Why do you say that?"

"Okay, here's where it gets weird. Mum said she was staying at this place."

"Did you speak to the owner about it?"

Colleen nodded. "Not until this morning. I called several times over the weekend, but kept getting an answering machine. The owner never got back to me. When I called this morning, she answered and apologized for not returning my calls. I asked her if Maggie Murphy was available and she said no one by that name was registered. Then, I asked if Mum had checked out."

"What did she say?"

"She didn't. She seemed rushed and couldn't wait to get me off the phone."

"Did you text her a picture of Mum? Maybe Mum registered in a different name. Maybe that John Smith guy made the registration."

"I didn't think of that, but I'm not sure she'd want to share that information with me. I mean, it's private, right?"

"Yes, you're probably right. But you didn't answer my question. Did you text her a pic of Mum?"

"I did, but she didn't respond, so I called her again. This time she said that over the weekend she'd rented Melody Manor to three couples who were attending a class reunion on Saturday. They stayed from Friday through Monday morning."

"Maybe one of the couples was Mum with the new boyfriend?"

"Katz, pay attention. I texted a pic of Mum. The owner said the couples were in their forties."

"Then why would Mum tell you she was staying at Melody Manor?"

"'Tis a mystery that we need to solve."

"So, what's the plan?"

"I want us to go to the Melody Manor and speak to the owner in person. We'll show her more pictures of Mum. If that doesn't get us anywhere, we'll walk around town and put-up missing person flyers with Mum's pic on them. I've already created it and made copies."

Katherine shook her head. "I have to admit something doesn't seem right. Mum would have called or texted you when she arrived in Louisville. And, she wouldn't have given you the name of an Airbnb that she wasn't staying in. It doesn't make any sense."

"Please, Katz, I don't want to go alone, but if I have too, I will."

"It's not that I don't want to help you, but wouldn't your husband be a better choice to go? With his investigative background, he'd be perfect in finding Mum."

"Daryl doesn't have any time off because he took two weeks off last summer for our wedding. Besides, he thinks Mum is okay and that's she's having the time of her life."

"Or fighting for her life," Katherine said in a low voice. "Have you called the authorities in Melody?"

"I called the police department and spoke to an officer who took down my information. He's going to give it to the chief of police."

"Did he?"

"I don't know. He said the chief would call me but I'm still waiting for the call. When I asked to file a missing person report, he shot me down."

"What do you mean?"

"I got the impression he didn't take me seriously. He said that Melody has a very low crime rate and tourists are perfectly safe in his city. Then he said it didn't sound like Mum was in any kind of danger, that she was probably enjoying her newfound friend."

"I thought the police jumped on missing person cases. Did you get his name?"

"Officer Grant. Oh, and he said that if Mum was a minor or a person over sixty-five years of age, it would be a different story. But it wasn't a crime for mothers not to call their children every day." Colleen's voice broke, then she composed herself. "Daryl essentially agreed with everything the officer said."

"Even when you told him the officer, what's his name, didn't take you seriously?"

"Yes, can you believe it? Then, instead of assuring me that Mum was okay, he said that if the Melody police did find Mum, they didn't have to tell me where she is."

"Couldn't they make an exception and let her daughter know?"

"They can tell me if she's okay, but they don't have to tell me her whereabouts."

"I think that as soon as we arrive, we'll head to Melody's police department, that is if you haven't heard from the chief yet."

"Oh, Katz, does this mean you'll come with me?"

"Yes, but I insist on driving. I don't think your car is big enough for a large cat carrier."

"Thank you so much. I've been beside myself with worry. When can we leave?"

"I can't swing it until tomorrow morning. That will give you time to book us Melody Manor for a few days."

Colleen smiled. "I already did."

Katherine returned the smile. "Of course, you did."

"The owner was getting crabby about my questions, so I had to do something. Plus, she's the only Airbnb available for two nights that allow cats."

"That's a little off."

"What's off?"

"The fact that the place is available when everything else is booked."

"Maybe there was a cancellation?"

"And the fact that Mum said she was staying there over the weekend. Don't these two things raise red flags?"

"No, I think it's a coincidence, that's all."

"Hope so. Listen, I'll call you later with the time we should leave. I'll know more after I talk to Jake."

Colleen rose and hurried to the door. "Katz, you are the best! I'll call you if I hear anything new." She hurried out the door with Iris chasing after her. Katherine intercepted the cat before she ran outside. She snatched the rowdy feline. "Where do you think you're going, Miss Siam?"

"Yowl," Iris sassed in a muffled voice.

Katherine looked at the cat. There was something dangling out of her mouth. "Drop it," she ordered. "Give it to me."

Iris dropped a shiny object on the floor and bounded up the stairs three at a time.

Colleen rang the doorbell.

Katherine picked up Iris's prize — a key ring with a shamrock charm attached to it — and rushed to open the door. "I think these belong to you?"

"I'll be needing those," Colleen grinned. "Mum gave me the lucky charm last summer. They must have fallen out of my purse."

Katherine laughed. "You mean they were stolen out of your purse. Iris strikes again."

"That cat!" Colleen said, taking the keys.

"I hope the charm brings us luck in finding Mum."

Tears welled in Colleen's eyes. "I pray they do too," she said, leaving.

Chapter Two

Later in the afternoon, Katherine crammed her clothes in one bag and packed enough cat provisions to last a few days. She loaded a litterbox and cat litter in her Subaru Outback, but waited to finish packing until the next morning before she left. Jake was teaching a class at three and wouldn't be home for another hour, so Katherine walked over to Stevie's and Salina's house so she could tell them where she was going. She could have texted, but she had an ulterior motive. She wanted to see the black kitten, Intruder, whom Stevie had taken in after Rachael left town.

She noticed that Stevie's van for his electric contracting business wasn't in the driveway, but she knew Salina would be home from school. Salina opened the door on the second knock.

"KC," she said excitedly. Salina nicknamed Katherine KC because she said Katz sounded too much like cats, and whenever she said it, the Siamese thought she was talking about them. "What brings you over here?" She held a black kitten in her arms. Wolfy Joe, an elderly gray cat, bellowed loud meows from the adjoining room.

The kitten reached for Katherine, who gingerly took her from Salina's arms. "I've missed you," she said to the cat, then to Salina, "She's getting bigger every day." The kitten purred loudly. "I came over to tell you I won't be home for a few days and to ask you a favor."

"What?"

"Could you look in after the cats while I'm gone? Just once a day after you get home from school."

"Where are you going?" the teen asked.

"Southern Indiana for a girlfriend's retreat."

"A what?"

"Colleen and I are going to a town in southern Indiana for two days."

"Where?"

"It's called Melody."

"Where are you going to stay?" Salina was an ace at asking questions.

"An Airbnb for two days."

"But won't Scout and Abra freak out while you're gone?"

"Yes, and that's why I'm taking them. So, you'll only have to deal with five felines."

"KC, did you forget? I'm going on my senior class trip tomorrow."

"Oh my gosh. I completely forgot it was this week."

"Five days in Washington, DC. My teacher says we'll tour the White House, go to museums, and eat at fabulous restaurants."

"I've never toured the White House, but the Smithsonian museums are excellent. As for dining in fab restaurants, how is your school going to afford that?"

"We have to pay for our own meals. My school is paying for transportation and hotel accommodations. Dad already gave me money. Oh, about Dad, he's going to an electrician's trade show in Chicago this week. He's leaving tomorrow."

Oh, that's news. How'd I get so busy not to know everything about you two like a nosy neighbor," Katherine teased. "How long will your dad be gone?"

"He'll be back on Sunday just in time to pick me up at the school when the bus returns from DC. I'm so excited. I've never been on a long trip before."

"I'm sure you'll have an amazing time. Who's going to take care of Wolfy Joe and Intruder?"

"Dad hired a cat sitter."

"You'll have a wonderful time. Take lots of pictures. Listen, I have to go home and fix dinner. Take care," she said, hugging Salina.

"I will, KC."

"Text me when you get back or whenever you want to text me." Katherine handed Intruder back to Salina, and left.

Jake pulled up in his Jeep Wrangler and parked in front of the pink mansion. Climbing out, he greeted, "Hello, Sweet Pea, what are you up to?"

Katherine rushed over to greet him. She hugged him and kissed him on the cheek. "I'm so glad to see you."

"Missed me, huh?" he kidded.

"Jake, I have something to tell you. I thought I'd give you a sweet kiss first."

"That was a sweet kiss. How about another one? I'm greedy."

"I'm not sure you'll want another kiss after I introduce the next topic. It has a bit of a sting to it."

"Okay, out with it," he coaxed.

"I know how you feel about Colleen's mother and that the two of you are not best friends, but she's gone missing and I need to help Colleen find her."

"Gone missing?" he asked, grabbing his briefcase from the Jeep's front seat and closing the door. He put his arm around Katherine and the two of them walked up the sidewalk into the mansion.

Jake asked, concerned, "What's this all about? Maggie is missing?"

Katherine relayed every piece of information Colleen had told her, including the online dating site, the mystery man named John Smith, the historic town of Melody, staying at an Airbnb, and taking Scout and Abra. She waited for Jake's happy expression to change to a look of annoyance. When it didn't, she continued, "Colleen and I are leaving early tomorrow morning. I'm driving."

"To Melody, three hours or more from here? Why can't the police handle it?"

"Colleen spoke to an officer at the Melody police department who took down her information, but he's turning it over to the chief. Colleen's waiting for the chief to call her."

"How long has Maggie been missing?"

"Three days."

"Three days," Jake repeated.

"When her plane landed in Louisville, she was supposed to text but she didn't. Daryl said Colleen should sit back and wait to hear what the police have to say."

"I agree with Daryl. Maggie is a grown woman. If she made the adult decision to fly off to meet a man who she'd never met, then that's her business. Frankly, in this day and age, it's not safe to link up with a total stranger. Many women have been duped by online prospects of love and a relationship, then are bilked out of their life savings."

"I know it's Mum's business, but it's very unlike her to go silent and not answer Colleen's phone calls, texts or emails."

"You know how flaky Maggie is? She's probably having a great time, and for all Colleen and you know, she's back in Manhattan."

"Colleen called her brothers and they said she hadn't gotten back yet. They are worried, too."

"So why doesn't one of them fly out to help Colleen? Why does it have to be you? You know, Katz, Maggie is a danger magnet. She puts people in harm's way, including you and me. How do you know that

Colleen and you will go to Melody and not end up in the middle of a hornet's nest?"

"I don't think that will happen."

"What do you think will happen? You'll get there, find Maggie with this new guy, and give her hell for not calling. I think that's a pretty lame plan."

"I have a hunch that something terrible has happened to her. Colleen is very intuitive, too, and she feels the same way."

"If it makes you happy, by all means go, but I don't think it's a good idea to take Scout and Abra."

"Why not?"

Before Jake could answer, the Siamese trotted into the vestibule. Their tails were twice the normal size. The cats shrieked in a shrill, high-pitched tone, "Mir-waugh . . . waugh. . . waugh!" Abra began foaming at the mouth; her pupils were so dilated that they looked like black holes. Scout began her macabre death dance, arching her back and hopping up and down like a deranged Halloween cat.

Jake reached to pet her, but Katherine took his arm. "Don't. Let her finish."

She spoke to the cats in a soft voice. "It's okay, girls." She sat down on the floor and Abra came to her, collapsing in her arms. "Raw," the cat cried. Scout stood tall and started to groom herself.

Katherine said in a nervous voice, "Jake, now do you think it's a lame idea?"

Jake didn't answer right away, then said, "Nope, not after the Siamese just did their dance." He walked over and picked up Scout. "Your heart is racing a mile a minute. It's time to calm down, little girl." He began pacing the floor with Scout in his arms. "It's okay, baby girl. Just calm down."

Chapter Three

Tuesday Afternoon

Stevie Has a Lead on Rachael

Stevie drove his red Dodge Ram off the interstate, near Scottsburg, Indiana, into the parking lot of the 24/7 Breakfast Joint restaurant, and turned off the engine. He sighed and thought about the reason for this three-hour trip to southern Indiana, and it wasn't to attend an electrician's trade show in Chicago. He felt guilty for lying to his daughter about where he was going, but knew that she wouldn't approve. She wasn't a fan of Rachael, but he hoped one day she would be. Besides, Salina couldn't keep a secret if she tried. The last thing Stevie wanted was to find Rachael and then have Salina announce it on social media like she did before, when she alerted the world to Rachael's whereabouts. Her Internet video went viral and brought the mob to Erie, where two Erie police officers were shot. Stevie thought, *No, I won't tell her. It's too risky. If I find Rachael, I'll tell her then.*

Last July, when Rachael entered the Witness Protection Program, Stevie was resigned to the fact that he would never see her again. But when the main mob principals were deceased or put behind bars for life, he regained some hope that the couple could be together. The program allowed contact between loved ones through an intermediary contact and address. Stevie had written several letters to Rachael, but she never replied. He wondered if she'd lost interest in him.

Before Rachael was whisked off by FBI agents, she gave him her grandmother Pearl's number at the assisted living facility in New York City. She told him not to contact her beloved Grammy unless it was an emergency, and to use a burner phone so there wasn't any chance of the mob finding out where her grandmother lived. It wasn't a dire emergency, but Stevie called anyway. It turned out to be another dead end in his quest to find Rachael. Her grandmother had passed away.

Then Stevie got a Facebook friend request from a man he had served time with at the state penitentiary in Michigan City. When Stevie was released on parole, Smitty was still serving his time, but recently was transferred to his home town in Melody, Indiana, where he finished his sentence in a work release program. Stevie readily accepted the friend request and the two began emailing each other.

Smitty needed advice on starting his own electric contracting business, and Stevie needed someone to talk to about Rachael. Stevie sent him a picture of Rachael, and Smitty wrote back that he thought she was gorgeous. He also asked for his cell number and the two exchanged numbers.

When Smitty called Stevie, he answered on the third ring, "Hey, Smitty. How's it going?"

"Pretty good. Thanks for that info you sent me. It really helped. Listen, the reason why I'm calling is that I think I saw your gal."

"Rachael?"

"Yeah, man. I swear it was —"

Stevie cut him off, "Where did you see her?"

"She's a waitress at this restaurant outside of town."

"Melody, you mean?"

"Yeah."

"What's the name of it?"

"Rusty's Roadhouse."

"Where is it?"

"A few miles west of town on the main drag. You can't miss it. It's got a big neon sign out front."

"How do you know it was her?"

Smitty paused, then said, "I took a lady friend out to dinner at the roadhouse. Our server was the spittin' image of Rachael."

"Did you say anything to her?"

"Hey wait. I've got another call coming in. Hold on."

Stevie waited for several minutes before Smitty came back on the line. When he did, he asked again, "Did you say anything to her?"

"Yep, I asked her if she was Rachael."

"What she'd say?"

"She didn't say a word because my dumbass date chimed in and said, "She can't be Rachael because her name tag says Sally."

"Then what happened?" Stevie was getting annoyed at how long it was taking Smitty to tell him the facts.

"The waitress turned beet red, left, and sent someone else back to the table to take our order."

"When was this?"

"Last Saturday."

"Have you been back to the restaurant?"

"Nope. Can't afford it. It's kind of pricey."

"Okay, thanks so much. I'll check it out."

Smitty wasn't finished with his part of the conversation. "I wanted to take her picture and text it to you, but my date was pissed at me for looking at other women."

"No problem."

"Hey, if you come to town, be sure to look me up."

"I'll do that."

"We'll have a few beers. Hey, man, I hope you find her."

"Me, too."

Stevie hung up with mixed emotions. Could he trust Smitty to tell him the truth? He hardly knew him and didn't know how honest he was. Was this some kind of pretext to get him to Melody, so he could ask for more help starting his business? Or did Smitty see someone who resembled Rachael? He hated the idea of driving for hours to find out Smitty was wrong.

After weighing the options, Stevie decided to check it out. His mission was to see if this woman was the love of his life. If she wasn't, he'd get back on the road and drive to Chicago to the trade show he was slated to attend.

Stevie got out of the truck, stretched his legs, went in and bought a cup of coffee. Drinking it, he returned and plugged in the address of the roadhouse on his GPS device. Rusty's Roadhouse opened in the morning at nine and didn't close until midnight. He planned to get there as soon as he could. He hoped he'd find her right away, so he wouldn't appear suspicious by hanging out there all day. *I pray she's there*, he thought. *Because if she isn't, I don't know if I can go on this way, thinking about her constantly, worrying about her, and wanting to hold her in my arms again.*

Stevie turned the key in the ignition and the truck wouldn't start. Judging by the clicking sounds coming from the starter, he knew he either needed a new battery or a new starter. "Damn," he cursed the truck. "You picked a fine time to conk out on me. How am I supposed to find a mechanic at this time of the day?" He did a Google search, found a nearby car dealership, and called their number. The woman in the service department said they could tow his truck in for the repair, but the mechanic couldn't get to it until the next morning. After he described the truck and said he was at the 24/7 Breakfast Joint restaurant, she said she'd send someone right away.

"Perfect," he said. "Thanks so much. Should I call you tomorrow morning to check on the repair?"

She answered, "Yes, by all means. My name is Rachael."

"Rachael?" Stevie asked, surprised.

"Yes, I was named after my grandmother."

"That's nice."

"And because you've been so nice," the woman gushed, "I'll put a rush on your repair so your truck can be fixed as soon as possible."

"Thank you. I appreciate it so much."

"In fact, maybe one of the guys can fix it today," she continued in a flirty voice.

"That would be wonderful. Take care now," he said, hanging up. Stevie remembered that in previous days before he'd met Rachael, he could easily pick up this woman, but shook his head. "Those days are over," he said aloud. "And how strange it was that the woman's name was Rachael." He frowned. "I'm bankin' the truck won't be finished until tomorrow morning. I have to wait another day to see if the woman in Melody is really my Rachael."

Chapter Four

Road Trip to Melody, Indiana

Tuesday Afternoon

Katherine sat behind the steering wheel of her Outback and set the windshield wipers to full force. Colleen was busy texting Daryl that they were almost to Melody. Scout and Abra were finally asleep in the carrier on the back seat. They'd screamed like banshees for the first hour, then passed out from vocal overexertion.

Scout woke up to the sound of pounding rain on the roof of the SUV and cried a worried "waugh."

"It's okay, Scout. We're almost there. It's just a little rain," Katherine assured the Siamese.

Colleen looked up from her cell and joked, "Yeah, just a bit of rain. Katz, it's raining cats and dogs." Then she laughed at her choice of words.

"So much for the weather app," Katherine complained. "Twenty percent chance of rain. Someone got that wrong. I'm glad we're only a few miles outside of town."

"Do you think we can stop for provisions before we check into Melody Manor? I'm starving. And if I don't have a spot of tea soon, I'll go into caffeine withdrawal."

"I vote we check in and get the cats situated in my room. Then we can go to the police department, forage for food, and maybe do a bit of antique browsing before we call it a day."

"In the rain? Katz, it's flippin' raining to beat the band. I don't relish the idea of browsing anywhere, but it would be a good opportunity for us to place my missing person flyers in the area."

"Did you bring your raincoat?"

"Ah, the saints preserve us. I forgot the flippin' thing."

"You're using the word flippin' a lot," Katherine noted.

"Well, it beats using the alternative."

"Raw," Abra agreed, waking up and running her claws over the metal gate of the carrier.

"Oh, here it is," Colleen said.

"Where? How can you see?"

"The town's entrance. Turn right." Colleen read out loud the message on the sign, "'Welcome to Melody—a historic town on the Ohio river.'"

"The place we're looking for is on Main Street."

"This is Main Street."

"Look for 413."

"Oh, there it is." Colleen pointed to the right.

Katherine double-parked and put on her blinkers. She leaned over and peered out the window. "Wow, that's a beautiful Victorian home. I think it's an Italianate. Kudos to the owner. It's very well-maintained. But where do we park?"

"Look, Katz, there's an alley running next to the house. Pull in there and see if there's parking in the back."

Katherine drove down a service road between Melody Manor and a large church building. In the back of the Manor was a small paved parking lot for three vehicles. A Mercedes was parked in one slot. A beat-up pickup truck took the second spot. Katherine parked next to it. She said to the cats, "We're here. We need to go inside and check in."

"Are we taking the cats inside or are we leaving them in the Outback until we come back?"

"I'm not comfortable leaving them in the vehicle. I'd like to take them inside. Can you help me carry the carrier?"

"Yes, I do remember having some experience with that," Colleen said, in reference to their girlfriend trip to the haunted beach by Lake Michigan and helping Katherine move to Indiana several years before.

Katherine grabbed her purse, opened the door, and climbed in the back seat to get the carrier. "Hey, Colleen, you push the carrier my way, and I'll jiggle it out."

Colleen tried, but the carrier was tightly wedged on the backseat. "I see that Jake loaded it," she muttered. "You and I would have made sure we could get the flippin' thing out."

"Now, now," Katherine admonished. "Jake was very helpful this morning, and, by the way, he was very understanding that I'm coming with you to look for Mum."

"Okay, understood," Colleen said, then added, "I'm so appreciative that you did. I was just teasing about Jake."

A woman in her late seventies with shoulder-length gray hair walked over. She was dressed in a ruffled white blouse and flowing red skirt. "Which one of you is Colleen Cokenberger?"

"I am," Colleen said. "Are you Mrs. Richards?"

"Yes, indeed I am." She moved over and shook hands with Colleen, then she addressed Katherine, "And, you must be the gal with the cats." She looked in the cat carrier. "I didn't know you were bringing Siamese," she huffed. "They are mean, spiteful animals. When I was growing up, we had a Siamese that used to chase us and bite our legs."

Scout hissed and Abra growled.

Katherine and Colleen exchanged concerned looks to each other and wondered if they had made a mistake by coming to this place. Scout and Abra rarely hissed or growled at anyone.

Katherine spoke, "Yes, I'm Katherine. You can call me Katz. I'm sorry about my cats' behavior. They're not mean in any way. I think they're tired and grumpy because of the three-hour road trip."

"Okay, then, but make sure they stay in your room at all times. I have a rule about unrestrained animals."

Katherine answered, "Understood."

Mrs. Richards turned on her heel and headed for the house. "Follow me." She walked to a side porch and waited.

Meanwhile, Katherine identified the problem with the carrier and unfastened the seat belt Jake had extended over the cage. Then, she unwedged the carrier and pulled it out of the SUV. When Colleen and she both had a hold of it, the woman called impatiently from the porch, "This way ladies."

The Siamese began shuffling from side-to-side which made the carrier difficult to hold.

"Quit it, you two," Katherine said in a firm voice. "Stop rocking."

The Siamese totally ignored the suggestion. They rocked more and howled their heads off.

Mrs. Richards opened the door to the Italianate. "Welcome to Melody Manor. Please, come in and follow me to the parlor."

Colleen backed in and nearly lost her grip on the carrier when she tripped over the high threshold.

"Steady there," Katherine advised.

The three walked into an enclosed sunporch with geraniums that grew out of clay pots on a plant shelf and on the floor, positioned in front of two tall windows. On the other side of the room, a door led to the inside of the house, and to the right was a large aquarium teaming with saltwater fish. The top was partially covered with a metal shelf for fish food.

Scout and Abra caught sight of the fish tank and voiced their feline pleasure at the same time. Scout cried something that sounded like "yum."

Colleen giggled. "Katz, did you hear that?"

Katherine pretended she didn't and glanced at Mrs. Richards, who was standing at the door wearing a "would you hurry up" expression on her face.

"Now if we can proceed," she said impatiently. "This way," she motioned.

"We'll be right there," Colleen said.

"The parlor's in the front."

As Katherine and Colleen walked through the hallway to the front room, they stared in awe at the ornate crystal chandelier, damask wallpaper in shades of burgundy and gold, oriental traditional rugs, and the period piece antique furniture. A loveseat in the stairway alcove, upholstered with burgundy dyed velvet, was covered with magazines in various stages of decrepitude, from new to outdated. Heading to the parlor, they walked toward a double-doored front door, which was several feet from a tall staircase of varnished wood steps.

Katherine immediately noticed that the double-door had three bolt locks on it. One of them required a key to open. She asked, "May we use this door? It would be a lot easier for us to bring our stuff in if we could use this door."

Mrs. Richards shook her head and said abruptly, "This door stays locked at all times. One of my guests left it open . . . I mean literally open . . . and a homeless man made his way in and stole money from my purse. So, sorry about your inconvenience, but I never open this door."

Katherine gave Colleen a questioning look, but didn't say anything.

Mrs. Richards turned left into a Victorian furnished parlor, complete with two loveseats facing each other and a marble-topped coffee table covered with what looked like photo albums and Victorian-themed magazines. Various rococo side chairs with elaborate carving and curved lines were positioned along the periphery, with side tables matching their mahogany stain. The crystal chandelier overhead had one working light bulb in it and the wattage was very low. The velvet curtains were drawn, which made the room even darker.

"You can set the cage over there," Mrs. Richards said, pointing toward an inlaid tiled fireplace hearth. The artificial logs were ablaze in the gas insert.

"Waugh," Scout approved. "Raw," Abra added. They were heat-seeking Siamese.

Katherine set the carrier down and took a seat on one of the loveseats. Colleen stood nearby.

Mrs. Richards said, "I have paperwork for both of you to sign. This is a release form I have my guests sign, that states I'm not responsible for accidents that take place in my house."

"Could we see our rooms first?" Colleen asked.

"In just a moment. Allow me to finish. I have material for each one of you stating my house rules. Please read it as soon as possible." She handed Colleen a spiral bound booklet and moved over to Katherine to hand her hers. "I serve breakfast at 8:30. Not sooner, not later. The coffee pot will not be plugged in until that time. If you wish coffee before then, you'll have to walk to the nearest convenience store, which is just a few blocks down."

Colleen asked, "I didn't realize breakfast was included."

"Whatever do you mean? This is a bed and breakfast. A room for the night and breakfast."

"But your website says Melody Manor is an Airbnb."

"Semantics. Semantics." She waved her hand dismissively. "This is my home. I live on the second floor, so you can't have the place to yourselves. You must abide by my house rules. Is that a problem?" she asked, peering over her glasses.

Katherine read Colleen's expression and feared she would snap at any moment, then they'd be out of a room. "We're okay with that. Breakfast at 8:30 is fine. Thank you."

Colleen pursed her lips in annoyance.

Mrs. Richards turned on her heel. "Colleen, your room is next to the kitchen on the first floor. Mind you, that even though your room is close to the kitchen, you don't have kitchen privileges, which means do not take anything out of the refrigerator, use the stove or microwave."

"No problem there," Colleen answered tartly.

"And, you Katherine, your room is on the second floor. Go up the flight of stairs, then turn right. My room is on the left, but yours is down a long hallway on the right."

"Wait, maybe Katherine should have the room on the lower floor because of the cats."

"Whatever do you mean?" Mrs. Richards asked, which was becoming her favorite phrase to use. "The cats will do just fine upstairs as well as downstairs."

Katherine interjected with a fake smile (she was annoyed, too), "Fine, can I go to my room now so I can get the cats situated?"

"Why, yes. Your room number is four. Colleen your room is number one. Like I said, it's next to the kitchen. I'm going that way, so follow me and I'll show it to you."

"Could I have my room key please?" Katherine asked.

"Well, no, whatever do you mean? There are no locked doors here because too many of my guests were losing their keys. It costs a fortune for a locksmith to come every time someone lost their key. There is a sliding bolt lock on the inside."

Katherine gave a look of incredulity. She got up and struggled to lift the carrier by herself.

"Wait for me, Katz. I'll be back in a minute to help you."

Mrs. Richards stood at the doorway. "Chop. Chop. I don't have all day. I have a bed and breakfast to run."

Colleen's eyes grew large with indignation. When Mrs. Richards was gone, she mouthed the words, "What is it with this woman?"

Katherine shrugged, then said, "Hurry up and get back here to help me. I don't think I can manage carrying the cats upstairs by myself."

After Colleen had left the room, Katherine moved over to the cat carrier and looked inside. Scout and Abra were curled up fast asleep.

Katherine didn't wake them, but took the opportunity to leave them in the parlor and to head upstairs to cat-proof their room for the next two nights. That meant looking all over for any object that could hurt them if eaten or batted around.

When she exited the parlor, she studied the front doors. The bolt lock with a key was keyless, which meant Mrs. Richards had the key in her possession. She muttered, "How do I get out of here if there's a fire?" She mentally put it on her list to ask the owner.

The front vestibule was very dark. She searched for a light switch, but when she turned it on, the above ceiling light didn't work. She looked for a table lamp, found one and turned it on. It didn't work either. She made a second note to use her cellphone's flashlight every time she went up and down the stairs.

Using the handrail for safety, Katherine climbed the steep stairs. She found her room at the end of the hall and turned on the stained-glass lamp sitting on the table next to the entrance. She stopped and said out loud, "But wait a minute. She was serious about there not being an external lock on the door." She wasn't happy about this and logged in another question to ask Mrs. Richards.

Inside her room, she switched on the overhead light. The light flickered several times, then came on. She moved to an ornate rococo dresser and turned on the lamp there. The bulb hardly cast a light in the dark room. She found another lamp by the bed on a bedside table, she engaged that one, too. It worked, but the bulb was very dim.

The only decent lighting came from the bathroom, which had a light fixture with three bulbs in it. She turned that on, and it cast enough light through the doorway, so she could look under the bed, under chairs, and other pieces of furniture in her mission to cat-proof.

Not finding anything that would hurt the cats, she was just about to go back downstairs when she saw the panel next to the bathroom sink. It was recessed into the wall with two antique wingnuts holding it in place. When she tested it to see if a cat could pry it off, one of the wingnuts fell and the panel flipped open. Inside was a cavernous dark hole leading to parts unknown. Katherine used her cell's flashlight to look inside. Foam insulated pipes ran vertically in the space. She made another note of something to ask Mrs. Richards. Hastily she picked up the wingnut and screwed it in place as best as she could without a screwdriver.

Colleen called from the end of the hall, "Where are you?"

"Oh, I'm here," Katherine said, meeting her halfway. "Does your door have a sliding bolt lock on the inside?"

"I don't know. I didn't look."

"It's held on by four screws. Any criminal can kick the door in."

"Thanks, Katz. Now I won't be able to sleep all night."

"What about an exterior lock? Does your door have one?"

"Nope. I guess she meant what she said."

"So, we can't lock our doors while we're out?"

"I know. We'll have to leave our valuables locked up in your vehicle."

"But what about the safety of Scout and Abra when I'm not here?"

"Oh, I didn't think about that. What can we do?"

"Not sure, but since both of us being former New Yorkers, with safety always on our minds, we know this place isn't secure."

"Maybe we could drive to a hardware store and buy those prop things you lean against the doorknob."

"But how is that going to help us secure our room from the outside?" Katherine asked, worried.

"I'm sorry, Katz. If there was any other place to stay, we'd be out of here. But there isn't."

Katherine, still annoyed, said, "I was counting on having the place to ourselves. Why would someone advertise their B&B as an Airbnb?"

"I think she's a bit daft."

"You may be right. Okay, with that said, let's bring up the cats before they cook themselves in front of the fireplace."

"Sounds like a plan."

"After we unload the SUV and the cats are settled, we'll go to the police station. You have the address, right?"

"Yes, it's not far from here. It stopped raining. We could actually walk."

"That's even better. I need to get my steps in."

Chapter Five

Late Tuesday Afternoon

Katherine and Colleen left Melody Manor and walked down Main Street to the town's thriving shopping district, which was confined to a four-block area. Each side of the street was lined with two-story storefronts built in the 1880s. It was a mecca of different businesses, ranging from restaurants to antique stores to novelty shops. A steady throng of tourists and locals made walking on the sidewalk difficult.

"Obviously the rain hasn't deterred people from shopping," Katherine observed.

"Can't blame them. A little bit of retail therapy doesn't hurt anyone."

"Hey, look, there's the police station." Katherine pointed.

The building was at the end of a block of similar-looking storefronts, but had its own parking lot on the side. In order to get to the station, Katherine and Colleen dodged a mother pushing a baby stroller with her four kids meandering around her. They found the entrance and walked in.

Colleen approached the front desk, while Katherine stayed behind. A tall, stocky officer with short-cropped black hair asked, "Can I help you?"

Colleen stepped over. "My name is Colleen Cokenberger. I called yesterday morning about my mother being missing. Her name is Maggie Murphy."

"Oh, yes, I remember. I took down your information. What can I do for you?"

Colleen glanced at his name tag, then said, "Officer Grant, I would like to talk to the chief of police."

"The chief has received your paperwork. She should be calling you shortly."

"Sir, it's been over twenty-four hours and she hasn't contacted me. Is there someone else I can speak to about this?"

"You need to go home and wait for the chief to call you," he repeated in a commanding voice.

"It's not a matter of going home. We just drove three hours to get here."

"I don't have your paperwork in front of me. How long has your mother been missing?"

"Since Friday night."

"Okay, take a seat. I'll see what I can do." He motioned for the two to take seats in front of a large picture window.

Colleen fidgeted in her seat and said impatiently, "Why do I think this is a dead end coming here, with that officer over there, planning on when he can eat his next donut, will probably tell me to go home again?"

Katherine hushed her, and whispered, "I think it's a stereotype to assume the police are addicted to donuts. He's big and stocky, not as big as a bus."

"Whatever," Colleen answered, extracting her phone from her purse. She began logging into the bank account she shared with her mother.

"What are you looking at?" Katherine asked nosily.

"I've been trying to get in Mum's bank account to see if she's made any charges."

"Trying?"

"Yes, for days. When I didn't hear from her Friday night, I logged into the bank's computer, and punched in the wrong password. When I tried another one, the computer kicked me off. Then I waited until Saturday, logged in, and changed my password. When I got the text with the code to change it, I created a new password, but I still couldn't get the flippin' thing to work."

"Maybe you should call the bank. Maybe Mum has left a digital trail of where she's been and used the card. Not that it's any of my business, but I didn't realize you shared a bank account with Mum."

"It's a joint checking account. I never use it. It's Mum's money, but I can make deposits, in case she's hard up for cash, which fortunately she hasn't been."

"Hey look, I think the officer is talking to someone on the phone. Maybe he's trying to find someone for us to talk to."

Colleen began to speak anxiously, "Eureka. I got on. Let's see. Okay, here it is. Mum made a debit charge at an airport kiosk at 9:45 p.m."

"Louisville Airport, right?"

"Yeah."

"That's good news, but are there any other charges after that?"

Colleen looked back at her phone. "Oh, bloody hell, Katz. She withdrew a thousand dollars."

"What? Why? Where?" Katherine asked in rapid-fire succession.

"At three different ATM machines."

"In Louisville?"

"Yes. At the airport."

"This doesn't make any sense to me."

"I know. Me either. Now I'm freaking out."

"Calm down there, girlfriend. Maybe Mum planned on doing some shopping in Melody, or she was going to pay for her room in cash."

A slender, middle-aged woman with a bleached-blond short haircut, wearing dark blue police attire, walked out of an office and came over. "Hello, which one of you is Colleen Cokenberger?"

Colleen looked up from her phone. "'Tis me."

"Would you follow me to my office?"

"Can my friend come, too?"

"As you wish." She directed Colleen and Katherine into a small, cluttered room. "Please take a seat."

They sat down on torn leather chairs.

Katherine noticed the chief's vintage metal desk was a total mess and did a side glance at Colleen. Both were neat freaks. On the right side of the desk was a tall stack of file folders. The landline phone looked like a candidate for a museum. The older Dell computer consumed the rest of the desk. Post-it-notes in different colors lined the monitor. In each corner of the room were books and 3-ring binders stacked knee-high on the floor.

The officer introduced herself, "I'm Chief Merrill. Officer Grant tells me you've driven three hours to inquire about the whereabouts of your mother. I hope I haven't wasted your time," she said, sitting down.

"Dead end," Colleen mumbled, frustrated.

"Miss, I understand your worry. I know I'd be worried if my mother was missing, but my hands are tied."

"What do you mean?" Colleen asked.

"We have no proof that your mother is in Melody or ever came here."

"But she said she was staying at a bed & breakfast close to town."

"Which one? We have several."

"Melody Manor."

"Okay, have you talked to anyone at Melody Manor?"

"Yes, but the owner, Mrs. Richards, said my mother never registered, never showed up."

"You told Officer Grant that last Friday your mother flew to Louisville and that you haven't heard from her since."

"Yes. I have proof that she landed in Louisville because she used our joint debit card at a kiosk at the airport."

"Joint debit card?"

"It's my mother's bank account. My name is also on the account, but I never touch the money."

The chief continued, "The simple fact is Louisville is in Kentucky and Melody is in Indiana. We don't have jurisdiction in cases occurring in a different state."

"But I'd swear she came to Melody. That she's here now."

"Why do you think that?"

Colleen began citing the facts as she knew them. "My mother met a man online from Melody. His name is John Smith. He asked her to spend the weekend here."

"Okay, let's backtrack. You said online? I presume a dating site?"

"Yes. I don't know the name of it."

"And, your mother lives where?"

"She rents an apartment in Manhattan."

"So, your mother, who lives in New York, flew to Louisville to meet a man she met on the Internet. How was she going to get to Melody? It takes over an hour to drive from the airport to here."

"I don't know how she was going to get here. My mother doesn't like to take a train or a bus, so she probably hired a car service. Or maybe John Smith met her flight and he drove her to Melody."

"When was the last time you heard from your mother?" the chief asked.

"Last Friday. She texted me from LaGuardia Airport."

"Did she offer any information on the man she was meeting?"

"Just that his name was John Smith and he had a business in Melody."

"What kind of business?"

"I didn't ask and she didn't say."

"Is it usual for your mother to keep you informed of her every movement?" the chief asked matter-of-factly.

Colleen was caught off-guard. "Yes, we talk or text every day. She promised to call me as soon as she arrived at the airport."

"But isn't that what she did? She texted you she was at the LaGuardia Airport."

"No, I mean when she landed in Louisville."

"And she didn't call or text," Katherine added.

The chief seemed to notice Katherine for the first time. "And who are you?"

"My name is Katherine Cokenberger—"

"Are you two related?" the chief interrupted.

"No, we're best friends. My husband is Colleen's husband's cousin. But getting back on track, I've known Mum since I was a child and this kind of behavior isn't like her."

"Mum?"

Colleen answered, "That's what we call my mother."

"Colleen, is your mother on any kind of medication? Does she have any health issues, like a bad heart, epilepsy, or diabetes?"

"No. She's very healthy."

"Is she on illegal drugs?"

"Oh, no. Of course not."

"What about psychological issues? Does she ever take off and leave without telling anyone?"

Colleen shook her head. "Never."

"What about alcohol? Does your mother drink?"

Katherine answered, "No, Mum doesn't drink. She used to have a drinking problem but she attends the local chapter of the Alcoholics Anonymous in Manhattan—"

Colleen finished, "And she's doing just fine. That's one of the reasons why I check on her on a daily basis."

"How long has it been since her last drink?"

Katherine said, "Excuse me, but I don't think this is relevant. Shouldn't you be asking questions about John Smith?"

Chief Merrill shot Katherine an impatient look. "Actually, I pretty much know everyone in this town. There's old man John Smith who's in a convalescent home. Young John Smith has a family of five kids. I can't see him dating your mother—"

Colleen broke in, "Maybe he used a bogus name."

"Unless your mother told you what his real name is, we'll have to assume it's John Smith," the chief said sarcastically. "I notice a slight accent. Obviously, you're not from around here."

"I'm from Ireland, but I immigrated to the U.S. with my mother and my brothers."

"When was this?"

"In the mid-nineties."

"Are you a naturalized U.S. citizen?"

Colleen was taken aback by the question. She hadn't been asked this in quite a while. "Yes. Of course."

"Where do you live?"

"My husband, Daryl, and I live in Brook County. He's a deputy sheriff there. And Katz and Jake live in Erie."

"Katz?"

"That's my nickname," Katherine offered.

"You live in Erie," the chief noted. "Where's that exactly?"

"On the banks of the Wabash River about three hundred miles from here."

"Colleen, do you have any idea why your mother would be attracted to a man from the same state you're living in?"

"I don't have a clue. This is very unlike my mother. I can't fathom why she would take the trouble and expense to come out here to meet someone she didn't know."

"Sometimes when folks follow Cupid's arrow, it doesn't lead them where they want to go."

Colleen asked, "Can you help us?"

"I've taken down your information. I have your phone number, but I can't do anything. Legally, I can't start an investigation here when it seems your mother is in Louisville, or somewhere in Kentucky. Until I have hard evidence that your mother is in Melody, I can't do a darn thing. I strongly suggest that you call the Louisville Police Department."

Katherine realized they were getting nowhere with the chief. She stood up to leave, but Colleen remained seated. "Thank you for your time," Colleen said.

The chief stood up. "If you will excuse me, I have to be somewhere in five."

Colleen collected her bag and got up.

The chief ushered the two out of the room, then caught up with them at the front door. "Are you going back to Erie or are you staying here?"

Colleen said in a discouraged voice, "We're staying at the Melody Manor for two days."

"You're staying at the same place your mother said she was staying? Interesting. Is there a particular reason for that?"

Katherine volunteered, "Mrs. Richards allows pets."

"Okay, that's good to know. Good luck to you." The chief then walked back into her office.

Katherine and Colleen left. Outside Colleen said, "See what I mean? That was a complete waste of time."

"Not really. Now it's time for us to investigate."

"How?"

"We walk back to the Manor, get the flyers, come back, and post them. We go into the shops and restaurants and ask if anyone has seen Mum. Let's get started."

"But it looks like it's going to rain again."

"Yeah, you're right. Plus, with the crowd of people going in and out of the shops, buying things, it would take us a long time waiting in line to ask the owner the questions we want to ask. It's probably better to return first thing tomorrow morning when the shops open."

"Good point."

"Let's head back and get my vehicle. We need wheels to drive around and find a hardware store. I didn't see any downtown."

"Thanks, Katz. You're the best, but do you mind if I skip the hardware store and stay at the B&B? I think I'd like to take a little nap. Besides, I can check on the cats."

"Actually, that's a great idea. Maybe you could feed them, too. Their food is in my travelling bag."

"Okay, it's a plan."

Katherine stopped dead in her tracks. "Geez, what if they got out? Scout is Houdini incarnate. She can open doors, and with my door not having an outside lock, the Siamese could be terrorizing the B&B."

Colleen chuckled. "What a vision! I think you're overreacting. I'll check on them first. If there're any shenanigans I'll text you. But, don't worry. I'm sure everything is okay."

Colleen's phone rang. "Oh, hold on, I have to get this. Maybe it's the police." Colleen quickly grabbed her phone out of her bag and answered it. A loud, irate B&B owner was shouting on the other end. Colleen put the call on speaker.

"This is Mrs. Richards. Get back here quick. The cats were in my plant room and have knocked down several pots."

Katherine broke into a run.

Colleen said into her phone, "Stay calm. We're coming right now."

Mrs. Richards retorted, "Don't tell me to calm down. Those monsters are destroying my house."

"I'm sorry." Colleen disconnected the call and chased after Katherine.

While the two rushed back to the B&B, the chief popped her head out of her office and spoke to Officer Grant at the front desk. "Hey, Rudy, can you do a check for me?"

"Yes, ma'am," he answered, swiveling in his chair to face his computer.

"Check the hospital, the urgent care clinic, the morgue and the jail to see if a Maggie Murphy is a patient or inmate in any of these places?"

"I'm on it."

"Oh, and check to see if John Smith is still involved in the work release program."

"The one you arrested?"

"You've got it."

"Yes, ma'am. I'm on it."

Chapter Six

Late Tuesday Afternoon
West of Melody

Emma Rachael Thomas, now Sally Hinkley, the object of Stevie's affection and former cat wrangler of Scout and Abra, drove her used Mazda down a gravel road outside of Melody, Indiana. She saw the old oak tree on the side of the road where she could park and take a walk down the farmer's service road. She'd met the farmer once, and he gave her permission to take as many walks as she wanted, but advised her to beware of farm equipment, especially in the fall when he'd be harvesting the corn in the fields.

She'd been coming to this spot on a daily basis ever since the U.S. Marshal from the Witness Protection Program had relocated her to southern Indiana. The program had also found her a furnished studio apartment on the outskirts of town. It was close to Rusty's Roadhouse, where Rachael had found a job as a server. The Feds gave her enough money to get settled, but made it clear she needed to start making her own money to support herself. She had a little money left over from what the program had given her and bought an older model car. She hadn't used the money in the bank account she shared with her grandmother. She'd failed to disclose this information to the Feds, so she didn't touch the money for fear they'd find out, assume it was money she'd stole from the mob, and confiscate it. She didn't want to involve her grandmother in any way.

Rachael was thankful to the program for saving her life, but was not happy with the name they'd chosen for her—Sally Hinkley. She knew a girl by that name in elementary school who'd pull her ponytail every chance she got. But the program and powers to be didn't give her a choice in the matter, so "Sally" it was.

Rachael left the roadhouse at five and instead of going home, she drove to her favorite spot. It had rained all day and turned chilly, so before she got out of the car, she grabbed a sweater off the front seat and an umbrella just in case. Before she exited the vehicle, she looked around to make sure she hadn't been followed. She knew it was unlikely, because the road was a rarely traveled gravel road, and she'd see the cloud of dust from the road, which would give her time to get back in her car and get out of there. But since the rain had beaten down the dust, she'd have to be more vigilant and not stray too far from the car.

Rachael continued to be paranoid that the mob would find her, even though she knew the principals had been taken down, either by her testimony in court, which led to several incarcerations, or by the death of Ray Russo, her ex-fiancé, who'd taken his own life rather than go to trial. She still feared that someone else involved in the money-laundering website might come gunning for her. Because of her constant anxiety, she took great pains to keep her whereabouts secret, even to her new friend Ashley, who was also a server at the roadhouse.

Ashley was the perfect friend because she never asked personal questions. She also loved to cook. She bragged that her family was from Italy and that's why she loved to cook Italian. Rachael had several meals at Ashley's house. She loved the experience, but most of all, she loved the cats.

Ashley took in stray cats, nursed them back to health, then adopted them out to responsible pet owners. There was one particular one named Shadow. She was an oriental shorthair with shiny black fur. Ashley thought she was about two-years-old, but didn't know for sure, because

Shadow was surrendered to the local animal shelter for being too noisy. Her friend found that ridiculous because Shadow was very quiet. Rachael loved to hold the sleek black girl and think about the black kitten named Intruder that she'd left behind when she entered the program.

Feeling secure that the coast was clear, Rachael began walking down the service road, looking at either side at the dead corn stalks, which reminded her of her own life. Once it had been vibrant, full of love and joy, but now her life was dying from disappointment and frequent bouts of depression. "Snap out of it!" she said to herself. "Don't dwell on the past. You have a new life. Make the best of it."

Her inner voice responded with its doom-and-gloom announcement, *Your Grammy is dead, the love of your life is gone, and that adorable kitten went with him, so move on. Decide what to do.*

"Oh, shut up!" Rachael said, then thought, *I was doing fine until that man and woman came into the roadhouse and he called me by my real name. I was so freaked out I nearly ran out of the restaurant. I thanked my lucky stars Ashley was off that night and didn't see my reaction and that another server took over my table without asking me any questions. Later he said the woman paid for the dinner in cash and that she'd left a generous tip. He was glad I'd asked him to take over.*

Rachael wondered what the relationship was between the man and woman because she appeared to be twice his age. Although she stayed out of sight while they were there, she caught glimpses. The man leaned into the woman as if she was the love of his life, but the woman didn't seem too interested.

Rachael's inner voice said, *If you leave the program, you can move to Erie and live happily ever after with Stevie.*

Rachael came to a halt and turned toward her car. She heard the loud muffler of a vehicle approaching. She hurried back, got in and started it up. The vehicle drove by, then stopped, backed up behind her and blocked her way of getting out. Rachael panicked. "Who is it?" She checked the sideview mirror and realized it was her friend Ashley driving her older model Cherokee. She hurried out of the car to talk to her.

Ashley powered down her window. "Girl, I've been trying to get ahold of you since you left the restaurant. You need a cellphone."

"I don't need a cellphone. I have a landline."

"I know. I called and called and kept getting your answering machine, so I hopped in my car and came looking for you."

"How'd you find me?"

"Duh, you said you liked to walk in some field by the big old oak tree. Everyone in Melody knows where that tree is," Ashley laughed.

"Okay, you found me. What's up?" Rachael asked.

"I'm so happy right now I could scream."

"What in the world? What's up?"

"Remember that guy I told you about? The one I met online on the dating site?"

Rachael moved closer. "You mean the guy you've been emailing? The one who wants to meet you?"

"Well, guess what?" Ashley said happily. "He asked me out."

"Good show, but how's that going to work?"

"He lives in Indiana."

"But where?"

"In Melody."

"No way. What are the odds of that?"

"I know. And, you won't believe this, I went to high school with him."

"Really?" Rachael asked, amazed. "That's cool. I'm so happy for you."

"You need to sign up on this site. I swear by it."

"I will," Rachael lied. She had no intentions of ever getting involved again. She loved Stevie. Plain and simple. "So, tell me more about him?"

"He's single, in his forties. He looks very fit in his online photo, like he works out a lot."

"Does he still look the same as he did in school?"

"He looks better," Ashley said, breaking into a wide smile.

"Have you two ever bumped into each other on the street?"

"No, after high school he moved away from here. He said he lived in northern Indiana and just moved back."

"I'm happy for you. By the way, what's his name?"

"John Smith."

"I was just about to give you the lecture about dating men you meet on the Internet, but since you went to school with him, I'll save the lecture for someone else," Rachael laughed.

"Yes, Mom," Ashley joked.

"When's your date?"

"Friday night. I'm meeting him at the pub."

"Which pub?"

"The one outside of town. The Juke Joint."

A loud clap of thunder startled the two of them. It started to rain and Rachael ran back to her car.

Ashley yelled after her, "See you tomorrow."

"Bye," Rachael said, getting in her car. She thought, *I just hope my friend's new love interest works out for her and that he loves cats.*

She drove to her apartment complex, pulled up to the community mailboxes, and turned her key in the lock. Opening the box, she saw a large manila envelope. It was from her handler at the Witness Protection Program. She rushed to her apartment, closed the door, and immediately opened the envelope. It contained two letters. One was from Stevie, which she dropped in a desk drawer with the other letters he'd written to her. She thought, *It's too painful to read them. The past is the past.*

Rachael's inner voice said, *Read them. You might learn something. Stop thinking of yourself and see how he is.*

"If I need your advice, I'll ask for it," Rachael said, slamming the drawer shut.

The second envelope was from her grandmother's estate attorney in Nyack, New York. Rachael opened it and found a copy of her Grammy's will. The attorney had highlighted in yellow the section that pertained to her.

A tear slid from her eye. "Oh, Grammy, I miss you so much." She wiped the tear with her sleeve, then sadly reminisced about the last day she'd talked to her beloved Grammy. It was hard to think about it because every time she did, she'd end up crying. She'd wished that the last thing they discussed wasn't about money, and how her grandmother had opened a joint checking account with both their names on it.

The attorney attached an instruction note and an affidavit form to the will. He wrote that there was a bank account—Rachael knew this was the one—which had a great deal of money in it. He'd already given the bank a death certificate for her grandmother, but the bank required that the account be closed, canceling the debit cards and temporarily freezing the money. The bank needed an affidavit signed by Emma Rachael Thomas to open up a new account in her name alone. He suggested that she sign the document and fax it to the bank as soon as possible. Once the bank received the fax, they'd notify him, he'd pick up the new debit card and FedEx it to her. The attorney emphasized that he needed Rachael's physical address to send her the new card and account information.

Rachael read the message twice before it registered. She had to sign her legal name and not her alias to access the money. Her inner voice interrupted, *Here's your chance. Now it's time to voluntarily leave the program. Grammy left you a bunch of money. Take it and start all over again.*

Rachael said aloud, "I wish it was that easy. I can't get the new card until I move to a different address."

It's simple. Move back to Erie and use your storefront address.

"But I gave the property to Stevie. What if he's sold it or rented it out to someone?"

You worry too much.

Chapter Seven

The Siamese Go Fishing

Katherine raced into the B&B's plant room while Colleen followed her. The two were momentarily speechless. The room looked like a tornado hit it. Several flower pots had been knocked over, with once thriving geraniums uprooted and scattered across the floor. Three clay pots were broken into large shards with black soil spilling out from them. The screened top of the aquarium lay on the floor with fish food scattered everywhere.

Mrs. Richards was standing next to the aquarium. Her face was flushed with anger and she held a broom with both hands. "Must I remind you of the rules? I have graciously allowed cats only if the cats' owner keeps them in their room. Those two Siamese terrors got out and ran throughout the house, bringing down such havoc I've never seen before."

Katherine assured, "I'll take care of it. Where are they now?"

"I don't have the foggiest. When I caught one of your cats fishing in my aquarium, I smacked it with the broom, and both cats scattered to parts unknown."

Katherine bristled. "You smacked my cat?"

"Why no, I didn't hit it. I just waved the broom at it."

Colleen pointed at the aquarium and asked solemnly, "Were there any casualties?"

"You mean, did that monster kill any of my beloved fish? Well, I don't rightly know, because I haven't counted them."

Katherine charged out of the room. "Scout? Abra? Where are you? It's okay. Let's go back to our room. Treat! Treat!" she enticed, running into each room, checking it, then flying up the stairs to her bedroom. She was surprised to find the exterior door closed. She made a mental note to ask Mrs. Richards if she'd shut it. Inside lying on the bed were two innocent-looking Siamese, striking a pose worthy of a cat magazine. Scout was washing her paw, and stopped her ablutions to squeeze Katherine an eye kiss. Abra cried sweetly, "Raw," which sounded like she was asking about her fur mom's day.

Katherine hurried into the room and closed the door behind her. "Okay, my treasures, that little stunt will probably get us kicked out."

"Waugh," Scout uttered, then hiccupped.

Colleen knocked and darted in. "Oh, the saints preserve us. Mrs. Richards is on the war path. She threatened to call the police."

"I think we better get out of here."

"But Katz, there's nowhere else to stay."

"If the police show up, they'll bring the animal control people and trust me, they'll take the cats. Do you want that?"

"Well, no, but . . . but . . .," she stuttered, pointing at the bed.

"What is it?"

Colleen eyes widened in shock. "What's that?"

Katherine turned to look and saw a dead fish on her pillow. "Eww. That's disgusting," she said.

"Is it dead?"

"Of course, it's dead."

Colleen gasped, still pointing. "Evidence! Evidence! Get rid of it quick!"

"Ma-waugh," Scout cried proudly.

"Bad cat," Katherine scolded.

Mrs. Richards pounded on the door. "Mrs. Cokenberger, I need to speak to you."

Katherine quickly grabbed a tissue, scooped up the deceased and ran to the bathroom. "Colleen, go see what that woman wants, but don't open the door until I flush the toilet," she said, then to the fish, "I'm so sorry. May you rest in peace."

Colleen opened the door slightly and peeked her head around the door. "Yes?"

Mrs. Richards advised. "I didn't call the police, but I will charge Katherine for the damages to my indoor garden."

Katherine came to the door and took over the conversation. "I apologize for my cats. I will pay double the damages. Is that okay?"

Mrs. Richards thought for a moment, then said, "Yes, but you must assure me those monsters will stay in your room."

"Please don't call them monsters. They mean the world to me. I'll take care of the damages. But right this minute, I have to drive to a hardware store to buy a security floor wedge to hold the door in place when I'm not here, because you don't have any way to lock it. I assure you once that happens, the cats won't get out again."

"But what about the mess in my plant room?" the owner asked indignantly. "I certainly can't clean it up myself."

"Once I'm back, I'll clean it up."

Colleen said, "I'll help too. Just direct us to the cleaning supplies and we'll have it cleaned up in no time."

Katherine asked Mrs. Richards, "Are you the one who shut the cats in my room?"

"Shut them?"

"I mean did you chase them to the room and close the door?"

"I did no such thing. I suffer from arthritis in my knees and I don't make a habit of coming up these stairs unless I absolutely have to."

"When I got here my door was closed just as I left it. My cats are exceptional, but they don't shut doors. Can you explain why it was closed?"

"No, and I won't waste any more of my time listening to this." Mrs. Richards turned her back and trudged down the hall.

Katherine called after her, "And don't ever smack one of my cats again."

The owner kept walking. "I *said* I didn't smack it. I scared it."

Katherine gave Colleen a worried look. "If she didn't close the door, then who did?"

"I think that daft woman chased them up here with the broom, then closed the door. She doesn't want to own up to it."

"What about her arthritis? I can't see her chasing after them."

"Arthritis? Pull the other one. She bounces around here like a spring chicken."

"If I hadn't seen the dead fish, I would question whether or not the cats even left the room."

"Yes, I must admit, the dead fish gave it away," Colleen noted. "I wonder how long it will take Mrs. Richards to realize one of her fish is missing?"

"I pray she doesn't notice, but I'll do some research to find out what kind of fish it was and reimburse her."

"How can you do that when you've already given the fish a toilet burial?"

Katherine brought her hand up to smother a laugh. "On my way out, I'll take a pic of the remaining fish in the aquarium who survived Scout's attack, then I'll text it to you."

"I'll Google it and let you know."

"Excellent, now let me go to the store. Can you sit with them until I get back?"

"Sure. No problem."

"Okay, see you in a few."

Chapter Eight

Wednesday Morning

Katherine was in a deep sleep. She was dreaming she was back in her old apartment in Manhattan. Scout was on the windowsill thumping her tail against the glass, clucking at the pigeons' outside. "At-at-at-at!" she cried.

Katherine called out, "Scout, quit it! Let me sleep."

"Mrs. Cokenberger, are you in there?" Mrs. Richards asked, while rapping on the door.

Scout growled and Abra hissed.

"This is Mrs. Richards. You are late for breakfast."

"What?" Katherine moaned sleepily from underneath the feather comforter. "Who?"

The Siamese leaped off the bed and bounded to the door. Scout reached up her long, brown paws and tried to turn the door knob; Abra remained on the floor and attempted to pull out the door wedge Katherine had inserted the night before.

Mrs. Richards knocked again. "Your breakfast is getting cold."

"I'm sorry. I'll be there in a minute," she said, then whispered, "I will if you stop banging on my door."

She got out of bed, saw what the Siamese were doing and scolded them, "Quit it. You're not leaving this room."

"Raw," Abra sassed. Scout flicked her ears and muttered a message only her littermate understood.

"Whatever," Katherine said. She moved over to the dresser to retrieve her cellphone. With fingers punching in numbers, she called Colleen.

Colleen answered right away. "Where are you?" she asked in a low voice. "I've been stuck talking to Mrs. Richards for hours. If she tells me again about the plant room disaster, I'll scream."

"I overslept. The cats kept me up all night and I didn't get any sleep. I'll be there in a New York minute."

Katherine threw on a pair of jeans and a long-sleeve T-shirt. She slipped on her shoes and hurried to the door. Removing the wedge, she said, "My darlings, I will be back in a little while, then I'll feed you."

The cats howled in protest. Abra began her "I'm starving" act and began rolling back and forth on the floor.

"Okay, let me edit that." She moved to the traveling bag, extracted their dry food, and scooped each cat a heaping scoopful. The Siamese dug into the food like they hadn't been fed in months.

On the way out, Katherine removed the door's floor wedge and hurried out. She put the wedge on the front of the door, made sure it was secure, then dashed down the stairs.

The breakfast was being served in a grand Victorian-themed dining room. Heavy burgundy-colored draperies hung from two tall windows, which flanked the center Rococo serving station where Mrs. Richards stood in front; she wore a Victorian-era dress and a pinched look on her face.

She'd decorated the table with expensive china plates, dainty tea cups, and silverware placed on a white lace tablecloth. Colleen sat at the far end of the table. Mrs. Richards showed Katherine to her seat and said, "I know Colleen prefers tea, but what shall you have Katherine?"

"Coffee, please."

Mrs. Richards lifted the silver coffee pot and ceremoniously poured the beverage and asked, "Cream? Sugar?"

Katherine yawned. "No, I'll take it black and I hope it's loaded with caffeine."

"Oh, my late husband drank his coffee black," Mrs. Richards began. Katherine didn't listen to her elaborate description of the late Mr. Richards, but thought, *I'm drinking it black because I didn't sleep a wink last night because two hyperactive cats wouldn't settle down for anything.*

Colleen was unusually quiet and didn't speak until Mrs. Richards left the room to get the food.

"What gives?" Katherine asked.

"Last night, I called the Louisville police department. I spoke to an officer who took down my information. She's going to do what she's got to do and will—"

"Let me guess. Call you?"

"Yes, and I hope it goes better than when I initially spoke to Officer Grant on Monday. We know how that went."

"Let's be positive. Maybe it'll go great and they'll find Mum."

"I'm sorry I vegged out last night when you got back from the store. I went back to my room, talked to the officer, then called Daryl. We had a long talk on the phone.

After that I hit me bed and was out like a light. I slept like I've never slept before."

Katherine gave her an incredulous look. "Perhaps you should sleep with the Siamese tonight, so I can get some sleep."

"You didn't sleep well?"

"Can't you see the circles under my eyes and my Medusa head of hair?"

Colleen grinned, looked at her friend's bed head, then said, "What did the little darlings do to keep you up?"

"They took turns trying to pull the door wedge out, then when that didn't happen, they went into the bathroom and tried to pry off the panel to the pipe chase."

"What's a pipe chase?"

"It's an access wall that the bathroom pipes run through. The panel covers the opening."

"How big is the opening?"

"About 12 x 12 inches."

"Just enough room for a cat to crawl through," Colleen joked.

"True, but as long as the panel stays put that's not going to happen."

"What's the panel put on with? Duct tape?"

"On the left side is a hinge and the other side is held shut by two double-sided turn buttons."

"How do you know this terminology?"

"I live in an old house, Carrot Top. I learn things."

"So go on, how do they work?"

"They both turn to open or close the panel. The screws were loose last night, so I tightened them the best I could."

Colleen giggled. "Maybe Scout and Abra think it's a dumbwaiter like the one at the old farmhouse you rented. They loved it!"

"I remember." Katherine smiled and finished her coffee. "What's the plan for this morning?"

"I think we should put up the flyers, walk around Melody, and ask about Mum."

"Yes, let's do this right after breakfast. I wonder what's taking Mrs. Richards so long. I'm starving."

As if on cue, Mrs. Richards came in carrying two plates that were heaping with an overstuffed omelet, covered with a white cheese sauce, and garnished with spinach leaves. On the side of the plate was a thick-cut slice of toast covered with creamy butter.

Katherine and Colleen dug in. When they finished, they went to their rooms to grab what they needed for their mission to find Mum. They met outside on the front stoop of the Manor. Katherine carried a small staple gun and a roll of tape, while Colleen carried a bag full of flyers. As they approached the heart of Melody, Katherine volunteered to be the *go-to* person. She'd walk into the business and ask if she could place the flyer in the window or post it on their community bulletin board, if they had one. After she did that, Colleen would explain that the missing woman on the flyer was her mother and ask if anyone had seen her over the weekend.

After entering each business on two blocks, Colleen said wearily, "We've been to almost every shop and no one has seen her. Maybe we shouldn't have come. Maybe Mum didn't come to Melody."

"I vote we finish our task, then figure out what to do."

Colleen pointed at the traffic light. "Hey, Katz, there's a walk sign."

The two hurried across the busy street.

"This place is a gold mine. I've never seen so much traffic in a small town, especially on a week day,"

Katherine observed. "Come on. We have two more blocks to cover."

"Would it be too bold to go to the police station and ask to put up a flyer?"

"It wouldn't hurt."

Katherine and Colleen walked to the police station. Colleen hurried in and approached the officer at the front desk. Surprised that it wasn't Officer Grant, Colleen asked, "Is Officer Grant here?"

"No, he's off duty. How may I help you?" the officer asked.

"We were here yesterday to talk to Chief Merrill about my mother being missing."

"And?"

"We wondered if we could put up this flyer in the window." Colleen handed her one, but the officer didn't take it.

"It's policy that we don't post material from private citizens. You can try the library. They have a community board. Also, the grocery store out of town has one."

"Could you please make an exception? I'm desperate to find my mother."

The officer glanced over to her computer and was reading something on her screen not related to Colleen's request. "Sorry. We can't help you."

"In that case, can you please give this flyer to Chief Merrill?"

"Yes, certainly."

"Thank you." Colleen turned on her heels and walked out. Katherine was a close second behind her.

"Wow, the officer couldn't even put the flyer up in the window," Colleen complained. "I think I would have better luck with Officer Grant."

"Why would you say that?"

"Because I'd offer him a pastry, and while he was gulping it down, I'd sweetly launch my question."

"Carrot Top, your police/donut notion is not going to get you anywhere."

"Why not?"

"Because it reeks of being a stereotype. What does your deputy husband think of your theory?"

"He says that every time I mention it, he wants a donut," Colleen said with a smirk on her face.

"Oh, geez. Let's pop into that café."

"Where?"

"Two doors down. The sign says Melody Café."

"I could use a cuppa."

"And I could use a donut," Katherine said cynically.

The two walked into a busy café full of locals and tourists sitting at tables covered with red and white checkered tablecloths. A server yelled from the far end of the room, "Seat yourself, ladies. I'll be right with you."

Noticing there were no tables available, Colleen and Katherine sat on stools at the bar. Colleen quickly pulled out a flyer. When the server came to take their order, she asked, "Have you seen this woman?"

"Who wants to know?" the woman asked suspiciously, not looking at the picture.

Colleen smiled sweetly. "This is my mother and she's been missing since Friday evening. She said she was coming here—"

"Oh, dear, does she have dementia?"

"No, why do you ask?"

"Because it happens. Older people get confused and wander off. Has she been like that for long?"

"Why no. She doesn't have dementia. Can you look at the picture and tell me if you've seen her?"

The server glanced at the picture and nodded. "Yes, I do remember her. Spoke with a funny accent."

"You do? When did you see her?" Colleen asked excitedly.

Katherine piped in, "What day?"

Two men wearing ball caps yelled from a table against the wall. "Hey, motor mouth, Holly, could we get a refill?"

"Who's talkin', Ken? Spread any lies today?" The server laughed, then spoke to Colleen, "I can't talk now. Give me your drink order and I'll come back as soon as I can."

"One black coffee and an Earl Gray hot tea," Katherine ordered. "And bring both of us a glazed donut."

The server hurried to pick up the coffee pot and headed over to the two men.

Katherine asked, "Can we trust her? She hardly looked at the picture. She seems like a flake."

"Daft or not, she just placed Mum in Melody. Now I have something definitive to report to the chief."

"The police in Louisville?"

"Yes, but most of all, the police in Melody."

"Go for it."

Within a few minutes, Holly, the server, returned with two cups and the donuts. She set them on the counter. "Like I said, she spoke with an accent and seemed to be frazzled about something."

"What do you mean by frazzled?" Colleen asked.

"Like she was drunk."

"Drunk? Did she come in with someone?"

"Well, you see, it was dark outside and the exterior lights in front of the café aren't that great. I could see a man with his back to the window. He never turned around so I didn't get a good look at him. She came in by herself. The reason why I remember her is that she came up to the bar and asked to cash a check. It was for a lot of money, so I went and got the manager who came out and told her we didn't cash checks."

"How much money?"

"Something like a thousand dollars. She said that back home, wherever that is, she'd cash checks at the bar."

Katherine commented, "Some of the Irish bars in New York cash checks."

"Oh, that explains her funny accent. She's from Ireland."

"Then what happened?" Colleen asked, leaning across the bar in anticipation of the answer.

"We told her no and she left."

"When was that?"

"Saturday."

"In the morning or evening?" Katherine asked.

"Evening. It was the end of my shift, say around eleven or so."

"Would you be willing to tell Chief Merrill what you just told us?" Colleen asked.

"Why yes, if she asks me. Now girls, I have hungry customers, so if you don't need anything else, I'll check on you later." The server walked away.

Katherine stopped her. "One more question. Do you have security cameras here?"

"No, the boss doesn't want to buy them."

"Okay, thanks."

"Katz, I *knew* Mum was in Melody," Colleen said.

"But now we have to find out if she's still here."

"And where she is. I'm worried that Mum has hit the bottle again."

"Me too," Katherine said. "Do you have a number for Chief Merrill?"

"Sure do."

"Call her and give her this information."

Colleen quickly went to her contacts list and scrolled down to the chief's number. The call went to voicemail, so Colleen relayed what the server had said. "Please call me as soon as possible. My mother is in Melody. This is a game changer," she said urgently.

After she'd hung up, Katherine asked, "Why would Mum use her bank card in Louisville to withdraw a thousand dollars, then come to Melody and try to cash a check for the same amount?"

Colleen speculated, "Maybe this guy was demanding money from her?"

Katherine shrugged. "I don't know. Maybe."

Colleen slid her plate with the glazed donut on it over to Katherine. "I really can't eat this."

"Why?" Katherine picked up her donut with its gooey glazed icing and bit into it. "This is the best. Are you sure you don't want yours?"

"Katz, I hate donuts."

Katherine rolled her eyes and looked up at the ceiling. "Who would have thought it?"

"I'm so bummed out right now. I could use a diversion. Can we browse some of the shops so I can try and take my mind off of Mum for just one minute? This constant worrying is wearing me down."

"I think that's a great idea. There's a shop two doors down selling Halloween decorations. Do you want to go there?"

"No, Katz, that's not what I had in mind. How about a shop that sells clothes? I need to buy fleece or flannel pajamas. It was glacial in my room last night."

"I could use a pair myself."

"Didn't the cats keep you warm?"

"Ha! Snuggling with their fur mom wasn't on last night's agenda."

Chapter Nine

Reunion

Wednesday Mid-Morning

Rachael hurriedly walked into the back of Rusty's Roadhouse and greeted her friend, Ashley, who was standing at the coffee bar making a fresh pot of decaf. "Good morning, sunshine," she said. "I apologize for being late."

"I'm so glad to see you. The lunch crowd has started to show up and the place is really filling up."

Rachael grabbed her apron out of a drawer and put it on. "Something came up and I had to run several errands this morning. Plus, I had a hard time finding a place that had a fax machine, but found one in the library."

"A fax machine? Whatever for?"

"I had to send something to a bank," Rachael said. She couldn't tell Ashley that the something was an affidavit which would allow her to claim the money her grandmother had left her. She wasn't sure of the exact amount, but if it was the money from the sale of her grandmother's Victorian home in Nyack, the sum could be over a million dollars. She didn't want Ashley to know about the inheritance because Ashley was struggling to make ends meet. It wasn't fair, but Rachael was sure of one thing, someday she'd help her friend.

"Oh, okay," Ashley said, biting her lip.

"You look guilty. What's up?"

"I hope you won't be mad at me, but there's a guy at table six who showed me your picture and asked me if you worked here. I said yes, that you were running a little bit late. He said he'd wait for you."

Rachael started to head out the back door.

"Where are you going?"

"I need to get out of here."

"What do I tell him?"

"Say I just called in sick and you aren't allowed to give out my number or where I live."

"He said his name is Stevie Sanders."

Rachael stopped in her tracks. Her mouth dropped in shock. "What?" she asked in disbelief.

Eddie, the part-time bus boy, came in carrying a load of dirty dishes. The simple fact of him opening the door scared Rachael, who thought the man at table six was an imposter working for the mob. She jumped.

Eddie laughed. "Hey, Sally, you look like you've seen a ghost." He picked up an empty bin and headed back into the restaurant.

Rachael sighed, then asked Ashley, "Describe him to me?"

"He's incredibly handsome. Tall, blond hair, with the bluest eyes I've ever seen," Ashley said dreamily.

Rachael felt like she was going to faint, then said, "Did he come in by himself?"

"Yes, about twenty minutes ago."

"Did he say anything else?"

"He showed me a picture, that's all. Why? Did I do something wrong? Was I not to tell him you work here?" Ashley asked awkwardly.

"You're fine. Look I can't go out there. Can you give him a note?"

"Sure, but hurry up, it's getting busy and if I don't get my buns out there, the cook is going to pitch a fit."

Rachael hurriedly scribbled a note in her signature flowing cursive. "What's the name of our kitten?" She folded it and handed it to Ashley. "Here, give this to him. I'll wait right here."

"But what about those hungry people out there?"

"Please do this favor for me."

"Sure, okay. It's the least I can do after spilling the beans that you work here." Ashley loaded up two cups of coffee and walked out of the prep room. She headed to Stevie's table. "Sir, I have a note for you."

Stevie stood up. "Where is she?" Without waiting for an answer, Stevie rushed back to the room Ashley had just walked out of, swung open the door, and stood in front of Rachael. He took her in his arms and kissed her passionately, then hugged her.

Rachael began to cry.

Stevie comforted, "It's going to be okay."

"I've missed you so much." Rachael caught her breath, then whispered, "I can't talk now. I don't want to blow my cover."

"Okay, when and where do you want to meet up?" Stevie said stroking her hair.

"I get off at five. My apartment is west of here. I walk home. Pull over and pick me up."

Stevie hugged her again, then said, "By the way, I love you."

Rachael smiled and fought back another round of tears. "I love you, too."

Stevie found the back door and left, not noticing the man parked nearby in a beat-up pickup. He'd been following Stevie ever since he'd gotten into town.

Chapter Ten

Wednesday Noon

Katherine and Colleen walked back to Melody Manor and sat down on two wicker chairs on the side porch. Colleen placed the bag with her new fleece pajamas on the third chair.

"I'm exhausted," Katherine complained.

"My feet are killing me," Colleen answered.

"My feet are just fine. I'm exhausted because of not getting any sleep."

Colleen ignored the comment. "I say we go to our rooms and rest for a bit, then start pounding the pavement again."

"Good idea. We need to find out if Mum has been seen anywhere else in Melody."

"We also need to find out what Mum did from the time her plane landed to when she went into the café to cash a check."

"That's twenty-four hours of missing time," Katherine noted.

"I don't understand why she didn't use her bank card. There's a flippin' ATM machine on every block."

"Have you checked your joint bank account again to see if she used the card since Friday?"

"The bank will text me an alert if the card is used. So far, Mum hasn't used it."

"I'm still thinking that Mum lost her wallet or her purse."

"But if she didn't have her purse, how would she have a check to cash? She always carried her checkbook in her purse." Colleen shook her head wearily and startled when her cellphone rang. She recognized the caller's name on her screen and quickly answered it, "Chief Merrill, thank you so much for returning my call." Colleen put the call on speaker so Katherine could hear it.

The chief began, "I've spoken to Holly Martin. She stated your mother came into the café where she works and tried to cash a check. Holly gave a positive identification of the picture on your flyer. I also talked to Holly's manager. He said after she left, he could see her join up with a man outside. He didn't know who the man was because he had his back to the café."

"Are you going to issue a silver alert?" Colleen blurted.

"Not at this time."

Colleen noticeably squirmed in her seat. "Why not?"

"Because I don't believe your mother is in any kind of danger. If she was, she missed her opportunity to cry out for help when she went into the café and tried to cash a check. She willingly joined the man outside who was waiting for her."

"But what about her not contacting me?" Colleen asked, through tears.

"The hard fact is, sometimes a parent will disappear and not contact their children. But nine times out of ten, it won't be for a long period of time. There was no evidence that your mother was forced into doing anything against her will. I want to investigate more. That's all I have to report. If you learn anything else, please call and I will do the same." The chief hung up.

"I can't stand this not knowing," Colleen sobbed.

Katherine got up and hugged her friend. "Let's go to our rooms and chill out for a bit. We both need to clear our heads."

"I guess so," Colleen said, standing up and heading to the door. "Thanks, Katz, for everything."

"We'll meet up in a few hours and go to the places we missed this morning."

"Good idea." Colleen walked through the kitchen to her room while Katherine headed to the front of the house.

Looking around for Mrs. Richards, and not seeing her, Katherine was happy she could have some private time. She walked into the parlor and sat down on one of the loveseats. She grabbed her phone and called Jake, who was driving home from his eleven o'clock class.

"Hey, Sweet Pea," he greeted. "How's my favorite girl?"

"Tired."

He chuckled. "Let me guess, the Siamese haven't been behaving?"

Katherine launched into an account of what the cats did and ended with the news of Mum being in Melody. When finished, she waited for Jake's comment.

"I never thought Scout and Abra would escape their room and cause damage. I hope the owner doesn't sue us."

"No problem there. I'm paying her double for the damages, which doesn't amount to much except replacing a few flower pots and plants. And I can't forget the dead fish."

Jake roared with laughter. "I know it's not funny, but fishing is what Scout has done in the past. She figured she'd have some fun while away from home, like a catly vacation."

"A catly vacation," Katherine repeated. "That's a good one."

"On a serious note, I'm glad you found out Maggie has been seen in town. Let's hope the police can find her now that they know she's in Melody and not somewhere in Kentucky. How much longer are you going to be staying there?"

"I want to come home tomorrow. Colleen booked the rooms for two nights, so after tomorrow there's nowhere else to stay unless we want to drive a long distance."

"Okay, I miss you and so do the cats."

"How are the kids?"

"They're fine, doing what they do best —"

Katherine finished, "Sleep in their cozy beds."

"Yep, except for Lilac. I've caught her several times hanging out by your computer."

"Really? Was there anything on my screen?"

"Nothing that makes any sense."

"Hit me with the best one."

"Basement waterproofing."

Katherine laughed. "I guess I have to be there for the cats to search the Internet and provide meaningful clues."

"I guess so."

"I'll let you go and concentrate on your driving. I love you so much."

"I love you more," Jake said, hanging up.

When Katherine climbed the stairs to her room, she was happy the security wedge was still under the door. She reached down and removed it, then walked inside. She stopped in fear. It was pitch dark inside. The two lamps she'd turned on earlier were turned off. Someone had closed the shutters and pulled the draperies shut. She'd remembered opening each one of them so the cats could sit on the windowsill and look outside.

Fumbling for the light switch, she flipped it on and gasped. The Siamese were nowhere to be seen. She panicked and began calling them, "Scout? Abra? Come to Mommy."

Abra ran out from under the bed and collapsed on her leg. "Raw," she cried.

Katherine picked her up. "What's wrong? Why are you trembling? Where's Scout?"

Abra jumped out of Katherine's arms and ran to the bathroom. The panel to the pipe chase was standing wide open.

"Oh, no, Scout," she called. "You better not be in there!"

In a few seconds, Scout climbed out of the hole and trotted over to her water bowl, leaving a trail of foam insulation behind her. She began lapping up water as if she was dying of thirst.

In a split second, Abra tried to lunge into the gaping hole. Katherine shut the panel, just in time, and covered the opening. Holding it in place, she rotated the top turn button to close it, then looked for the second one. It was missing. She got down on her hands and knees and began searching for the missing turn button. She found it in the bathtub. "I see you two have been playing hockey again? But where's the screw," she said to the cats, then to herself, "Just great! Now I have to go back outside, get my tools, come back, and screw this thing on more securely. And, if I'm lucky, find another screw."

Abra pawed the panel. "Raw," she cried.

"What's the attraction?" she asked, annoyed. "It's just a bunch of dirty old pipes."

Abra went behind the toilet tank and started clawing on the water line.

"Quit that," Katherine scolded, sliding over to take a look. There on the floor was a gold claddagh ring. Katherine picked it up and Abra tried to bat it out of her hand. "Where did you get this?"

"Raw," Abra cried sweetly.

"Okay, I get it, when Colleen washed her hands, her ring must have fallen off," she said out loud. She put the ring in her pocket. "Sorry, Abra, but this isn't a toy."

Scout trotted over and arched her back. She began swaying and screeching in a shrill, high-pitched tone, "Mirwaugh . . . waugh . . . waugh." Abra joined her in the dance, both of them screaming like banshees, in front of the pipe chase panel.

Not the death dance again, Katherine worried. "Girls, it's okay. Stop."

The cats screeched even louder.

"Shhh. Calm down. We don't want the owner banging on the door," she said, getting up and returning to the bedroom.

The simple act of Katherine leaving the room caused the Siamese to stop their macabre dance. They raced after her and jumped on the bed. It was then that Katherine noticed their cozy bed was missing. She found it on the chair nearby. Replacing it on the bed, she talked softly to the cats. "Are you okay?" she asked, petting their heads. Scout nipped her on the hand. "Ouch. Why did you do that?"

"Waugh," Scout cried, then smacked Abra on the head. This triggered a feline race around the room, finally ending back on the bed where it had begun.

"Why are you two so curious about the pipe chase? Are there mice in there?"

The cats ignored her.

"Fine, whatever. I have to leave for a few minutes, then I'll be right back."

"Ma-waugh," Scout cried, then licked Katherine's hand.

"Thank you. I prefer licks rather than bites."

Before Katherine left, she closed the bathroom door. "Do not try and get in there," she requested. She hurried out of the bedroom, closing the door quickly behind her. Once the door wedge was in place, Katherine walked down the long hallway to Mrs. Richards' door and knocked. "I need to speak to you."

There was no answer.

Katherine waited a few more minutes and knocked a few more times, then she started to leave.

Mrs. Richards opened her door. "Is there a problem?"

"I thought I made it clear that I didn't want anyone to come into my room but me."

"Understood."

"Why was my shutters and curtains closed?"

"Oh, my. I've been out and didn't have a chance to tell the cleaning lady. She tidy ups the rooms each morning. I'll make a note to tell her tomorrow when she comes."

"Yes, I'd appreciate it, but it hardly matters because we're checking out tomorrow morning."

"Oh, okay then. Is that all?"

"Yes, thank you."

Mrs. Richards closed the door.

Katherine said under her breath, "I wish I was checking out now."

Chapter Eleven

Wednesday Mid-Morning

Stevie left Rusty's Roadhouse, climbed in his truck, and started to back out of the parking lot. A beat-up pickup pulled beside him and honked. "What the hell?" he said, looking over.

The driver of the truck got out and came up to Stevie's window. "Hey man, I thought it was you."

Stevie smiled and powered down his window. "Smitty. Fancy meeting you here. You must be a regular at this restaurant."

"No, not really. It's too dang expensive. Whatcha doin'? Did you check out my lead? Was it her, your gal Rachael?"

Stevie wasn't too sure if he trusted Smitty or not. He'd found Rachael and he didn't want to share that secret with anyone, let alone an ex-con he hardly knew. He lied, "Nope, that's not her. You need glasses."

"Well, dang. I sure do apologize. Sorry you had to drive all this way for nothing. Will you forgive me if I buy you a drink?"

"It's a little bit early to be drinkin'," Stevie said. "I haven't eaten anything this morning. How about breakfast?"

"The roadhouse folks are serving lunch now, but I know a place downtown that serves breakfast all day."

"Where is it?"

"Downtown Melody. It's called the Melody Café. Just follow me. You can't miss it."

"Sure thing."

Stevie waited for Smitty to back out, then did the same and drove to the center of town. He turned into a diagonal parking space and cut off the engine. Getting out, he noticed a missing person flyer stapled to a telephone pole. He quickly realized he knew the woman in the photo and thought, *That's strange. I thought Maggie Murphy was in New York.* He read the blurb, then frowned. "Last seen in Melody."

Smitty walked over and saw Stevie reading the flyer. "Oh, don't pay any attention to that. It's just some old hag asking for attention."

Stevie looked at his friend and wondered why he'd made such a callous remark. He thought about texting Katz for more information, but quickly changed his mind. That would blow his lie to Salina about where he was. He changed the subject, "So, when are you buying me breakfast? I'm starving."

Smitty slapped him on the back and the two walked into the café. Holly Martin seated them at a table for two near the window. She asked Stevie what he wanted to drink, and when she took Smitty's drink order, she didn't establish eye contact with him.

Stevie noticed it instantly. After she left, he asked, "What's with that? What did you do to piss that woman off?"

Smitty laughed and said, "Oh, I had a date with her and she got drunk, then wouldn't put out."

"Love 'em and leave 'em, huh?" Stevie asked rhetorically. "I've been down that road."

"Speaking of that, I joined this Internet singles site and have already been on three dates."

"I thought those sites included women from all over the world. How did you find one in this neck of the woods?"

"Why do you ask?"

"Because our server appears to be from Melody."

"Oh, her? She was the younger sister of someone I knew in high school."

Holly returned with their coffee and set the cups down. Once again, she turned to Stevie to take his order. After he'd finished, she barely glanced at Smitty. "Next?"

Smitty said to her, "At least you could say hi to me. What gives?"

"What gives?" she repeated in an annoyed voice. "I would not repeat what you did to me in mixed company. Are you going to order or not?" Holly asked, getting angrier by the second.

"All right then. No need to be huffy. Two eggs over easy. Whole wheat toast. Two slices of bacon. And try not to spit in my food." He laughed inappropriately.

Holly gave him a dirty look and left.

Stevie said, "I won't ask you what she was talking about, so I'll move on to something else. How are you doing setting up your new business? Have you rented a storefront yet?"

"Oh, thanks again for emailing that stuff. I'm in sort of a bind right now. I realized it takes money to start a business."

Stevie nodded and wondered if his friend was going to hit him up for money.

"I'm working out of my mother's basement," Smitty continued. "I had business cards made and have been passing them around town. Things aren't too busy right now, but I think this winter things will pick up."

"May I make a suggestion?"

"Sure."

"You might want to invest in a better-looking truck. Potential clients notice these things."

Smitty cackled. "What's wrong with my truck?"

"It probably hasn't looked good since it came off the lot in 1980."

"Dang, man, I can't afford no Dodge Ram like you drive. And, the color. Seriously, red?" he asked sarcastically.

Stevie's face clouded, remembering that Salina had picked the color. He took a sip of coffee and explained, "If you bought a newer truck, you could have your company logo painted on it with your phone number."

"Oh, I get it. We'll see."

The bell jingled on the front door of the café and the chief of police walked in. She'd listened to Colleen's voice mail and was going to interview Holly. Looking around the room, she didn't see her, but spotted a face she didn't recognize. The chief walked over and sat down at the table next to Stevie's and Smitty's. She removed her tasseled hat and set it on the chair beside her. "Good morning," she addressed. "How have you been, John?"

"I'm keeping my nose clean, if that's what you mean?"

"Who's your friend?" she inquired, looking at Stevie.

Smitty introduced. "This is Stevie Sanders. He's here to help me start a business."

"What kind of business?" the chief asked.

"Electric contracting."

"Is that a fact. You should do well in that line of work. Folks around here are always in need of a good electrician."

"Ma'am, I feel I'm at a disadvantage here," Stevie said, smiling. "You know my name, but I don't know yours."

"I'm Chief Merrill."

"I'm pleased to meet you. I'm actually here to give Smitty some pointers about starting a business."

The chief looked at John, "So you go by Smitty now."

Smitty's face turned red and he looked down at his coffee cup.

The chief turned to Stevie. "Where ya from? I haven't seen you in these parts."

Stevie wasn't comfortable talking to cops, but he wore his best expression and smiled, "I own Stevie's Electrical. It's a business in Erie."

"Erie, you say?"

"Yes."

"Erie, Indiana?"

"Well yes. Have you heard of it?"

"Oh, you can bet your life on it. Sir, do you believe in coincidences?"

"I guess I do. Why?"

The chief pulled a copy of the flyer out of her pocket and flashed it in front of Stevie. "There's a missing person in Melody. A woman named Maggie Murphy. Her daughter and her friend are here looking for her."

Stevie said, "I just saw the flyer on my way in. I hope you find her."

Smitty was noticeably fidgeting in his seat.

The chief continued, "Mrs. Murphy's daughter is named Colleen Cokenberger. Her friend is from Erie. Her name is Katherine Cokenberger. Do you know them?"

"Yes," Stevie answered. "Katherine is my next-door neighbor. I don't know Colleen well, except to say hello to her on the street if we bump into each other."

"Interesting," the chief said. "How long have you been in Melody?"

"A few hours."

"Were you here over the weekend?"

"No, I was home with my daughter."

"I have a daughter. How old is yours?" the chief asked, making small talk.

"She's sixteen. She's a senior this year."

"Isn't that a bit young for a senior in high school? I thought most kids were seventeen, going on eighteen."

"Salina will be seventeen two months after graduation. She's the youngest member of her class."

The chief nodded, but didn't say anything. She addressed Smitty. "John, take a good look at this photo." She held the flyer in front of him. "Have you ever seen this woman?"

"No, can't say I have because I haven't," he answered, hardly looking at the photo.

"Did you have a date with this woman over the weekend?"

"A date," he said cynically. "With that woman? She's clearly not my type."

"Where were you on Friday and Saturday nights?"

"Helping my mom."

"On both nights."

"Yeah, and during the day, too. Why are you grilling me?"

"Because it has come to my attention that the woman in this photo, Maggie Murphy, had a date with a John Smith from Melody. Was that you?"

"Like I said, she ain't my type."

Holly brought the food over on a tray. She gave a wary look to the chief, then set the plates in front of Stevie and Smitty. "Will there be anything else?" she asked.

Stevie answered, "No, thank you. We're good."

After Holly left, the chief stood up and removed her hat from the chair. "Gentlemen, it's been good talking to you. John, tell your mom I said hello." She walked over to Holly and said, "Can we talk?"

"About what?" Holly asked apprehensively.

"About the missing woman in this picture."

"Oh, the lady in the photo? I talked to her daughter and friend. They were here about a half hour ago."

"Yes, they told me. Can you repeat to me what you told them?"

"Why, yes. I'll try."

Stevie strained to hear the conversation but couldn't. He wondered why the chief was asking them questions about their whereabouts on Friday and Saturday nights. Did the chief think the two of them had anything to do with Maggie Murphy's disappearance? He wanted to text Katherine for more information, but he was afraid she'd want to talk to him in person, and that would destroy his chance to hook up with Rachael. He decided against it. But one thing he was sure of. Smitty's body language would have raised anyone's hackles.

Stevie glanced at Smitty who was now wolfing his food down in big gulps. "Slow down. Are you in a hurry?"

Smitty swallowed and said in a low tone, "The chief and I go way back. She's the witch who put me behind bars. It was really hard for me not to jump up and put her in a chokehold."

"I'm glad you didn't."

"Why?"

"Because that would have messed up my breakfast experience." Stevie started buttering his toast, then asked, "Can you tell me more about this dating site? Do you have to post a picture or come up with some write-up about how much a hunk you are?"

"Hunk? That's girl talk."

"Just askin'. You get the picture."

"Yeah, you post a pic and give a brief bio."

"You said you'd met two or three women on this site."

"Yeah," Smitty answered, taking a sip of coffee.

"Since I didn't find Rachael, maybe I should post on this site and see if I can reel in any hot women."

"Forget the hot women. The good-looking ones are spoken for almost as soon as their pics are posted. I go for older women who look like they have money."

"Oh, so you want to be with a cougar?"

"What?"

"You know, young man in his forties with a chick in her sixties. Did you meet anyone like this?"

"Oh, come on. You sound like Chief Merrill. Why do you ask?"

"Curious, that's all. If you don't want to talk about it, fine."

"Nah, I don't mind. My date turned out to be a complaining hag. She bitched about everything. I drove to Louisville to meet her plane, then I took her to Rusty's Roadhouse and she bitched so much about the food, the service, and everything else under the sun that I made her pay for it," Smitty said snidely. "The woman had to pay in cash because she'd lost her purse at the airport."

"Why didn't you split the bill?"

Smitty kept laughing. "It was funny watching her fishing around her pockets looking for cash."

Stevie prodded, "Where was that woman from? New York, maybe?"

"Now why would you ask a question like that?" Smitty asked guardedly.

Stevie faked a smile. "Just curious. Since she flew in to Louisville, I presume you took her back there so she could catch a plane back home."

"No, I dumped her."

"Dumped her?"

"Yeah, like got rid of her. Never going to date that woman again."

Stevie's gut instinct told him that Smitty might have had a date with Maggie, but it was too far-fetched to believe. Why would Maggie fly out to Indiana to meet a man like Smitty? It made no sense. "When was this? Friday or Saturday?"

"Why does it matter?"

"Because you said you've already met someone else. That's fast work, my friend."

"Oh, I just thought for a minute you were an undercover cop."

"Why would you say that?"

"By the way you're asking too many questions."

Stevie laughed. "You gotta remember I have a teenaged daughter. I'm used to asking a lot of questions."

Smitty said, "I guess." He stood up and called to the server who was standing at the bar talking to the chief. "Holly, can we get some service here?"

Stevie could hear the chief say, "Thanks for the info. Can I speak to your manager? I want to get his take on things, too."

Holly walked to the back of the bar, poked her head inside a door and spoke to someone. The manager came out and joined the chief at the bar. Holly grabbed a coffee pot and headed to Smitty's and Stevie's table. "Do you boys want refills?"

Smitty sat back down. "I didn't know you were so chummy with the police. Were you talking about me?"

"You're not worth talking about to anyone," she snapped. She removed the bill from her pocket, slapped it down on the table, and walked away.

"Bitch," Smitty mumbled.

Stevie got up. "It's been good to see you, Smitty, but I think I'll head back to Erie."

"Leaving so soon? I thought we could get a few beers."

"Sounds like a good idea, but I really need to get back." Stevie grabbed the check. "And breakfast is on me."

Smitty said, getting up, "Got no argument there."

"Okay then, good luck to you." Stevie walked over to the cash register, paid and left the restaurant. Before he climbed in his truck, he snatched the missing person flyer off the pole, then drove off. He wanted to find a secluded spot where he could park and mull over what had just happened.

He also wanted to make sure Smitty hadn't followed him. He didn't trust Smitty as far as he could throw him. The man was guilty of something. He thought, *Maybe I was too obvious asking so many questions. But I can't stop thinking that he had something to do with Maggie going missing. If he did, I just pray he didn't kill her and dump her body somewhere.*

Chapter Twelve

Wednesday Afternoon

After Katherine had taken care of the loose screws on the panel to the pipe chase and spent some quality time with the Siamese, she walked downstairs and went to Colleen's room.

Colleen was standing outside the door, looking at her phone. She looked up and said, "Katz, I got a call from Chief Merrill. She wants to see me in her office as soon as possible. I was just getting ready to ask if you could go with me?"

"Yes, of course. Is there anything new to the case?"

"She didn't say."

"Oh, okay, I vote I drive this time."

"I was hoping you'd say that. My feet are still killing me."

The two headed to the Manor's back parking area and climbed into the SUV. Katherine drove into the police station's busy parking lot and found a space in the back of the lot.

Getting out of the vehicle, Colleen said in a sad voice, "I know it's bad news. That's why she wouldn't tell me on the phone."

"You don't know that. Think positive."

The two hurried inside the station and found a change of guard at the front desk. Officer Grant was back on duty. "Ladies," he greeted.

"Hello, officer. I have an appointment to see Chief Merrill," Colleen said with a worried smile.

"She's expecting you. Go right in."

Colleen and Katherine went to the chief's door and knocked.

"Come," the chief said, sitting at her desk reading something on her monitor.

Colleen was barely inside the room when she asked, "Have you found Mum?"

"No, not yet. Please have a seat."

Katherine sat down, but Colleen remained standing.

The chief said to Colleen, "It would really help my neck if you sat down, then I won't have to crane my neck to talk to you."

Colleen sat down and shifted in her seat to get comfortable.

"Katherine, hello," the chief greeted.

Katherine smiled.

The chief addressed Colleen, "I've talked to every business owner in downtown Melody. None of them have seen your mother except for the folks at Melody Café."

"Thank you," Colleen said. "We came back into town so we could speak to those owners that we missed this morning."

"You saved us some leg work," Katherine piped in.

"I have a few questions to ask. Before I spoke to Holly Martin at the café, I noticed one of our local regulars sitting at the table with a man I'd never seen before. I found a table by them and started a conversation."

Katherine set her purse on the floor and wondered where the conversation was headed.

"The man from out-of-town is a person of interest."

Colleen asked eagerly, "You found a suspect?"

"Well, yes, and I think I have probable cause to bring him to the station and ask him more questions."

"That's great. Who is he?" Colleen asked.

"I'll come straight to the point. His name is Stevie Sanders. Do either of you know this man?"

Katherine's jaw dropped. "What? Stevie Sanders?" she repeated.

Colleen said curiously, "Yes, we do, but Katz knows him better than I do."

"Okay, then, Katherine, when was the last time you saw Mr. Sanders?"

"I don't understand. What does Stevie have to do with Mum being missing?"

"I'm gathering facts. Answer the question."

"I saw him last week. He was blowing leaves off his yard."

"Did you see him this past Saturday?"

"No, why?"

"Did you see him Sunday? Monday or Tuesday?"

Katherine answered, "No, not on Sunday or Monday. I talked to his daughter, Salina, on Monday. She said on Tuesday he was driving to Chicago to go to an electrician's trade show."

"In Chicago?" the chief asked skeptically.

"Yes, Chicago. Why do you ask?"

"Because Stevie Sanders is in Melody. I met him this morning."

Colleen said, "That's impossible. Why would he be in Melody?"

"Does Mr. Sanders know your mother?"

"I don't think so. They've met a few times, but that was it."

"Did they meet on a personal level?"

Katherine interjected, "I can answer that. I think Stevie knows who Mum is, but I've never seen him talk to her or mention her in casual conversation."

"Katherine, what is your relationship with Stevie?"

"We are friends."

"Lovers?"

"Oh, heaven's no. I mean, we are platonic friends. Stevie has saved my life on a number of occasions, you can—"

"Okay, so you are platonic friends."

"You can ask Chief London about it," Katherine finished. "Stevie has gotten me out of a few life-threatening jams."

"Chief London?"

"Yes, he's the chief of police in Erie."

"Yes, I'm aware of that. I'll cut right to the chase. Do you think Stevie cooked up a scheme to kidnap Maggie Murphy?"

"Absolutely not."

"Can you explain that further? Why is it that a man from Erie is in Melody the same time you and Colleen are here?"

"It's purely a coincidence."

The chief shook her head. "In my profession, I don't believe in coincidences."

"I don't know why he's here. His daughter said he was in Chicago this week. Honestly, that's all I know."

"I've done some preliminary investigation on you, Katherine. You've had some unpleasant things happen to you since you moved from New York. Several assaults and murders in your house."

Katherine gave Colleen a "What's happening here?" look.

"You inherited quite a bit of money and your net worth is in the millions."

"So, what has this to do with anything?" Katherine asked, getting annoyed, wondering if she should walk out and call her attorney.

"Does Stevie Sanders know you are worth millions?"

"I assume so, everyone in town knows it," Katherine answered.

"Has he ever spoken to you about it?"

"Never."

The chief switched gears and asked Colleen, "Do you think Stevie would lure your mother to Melody to hold her for ransom—"

Colleen butted in, "'Tis insane. If that was the case, and I'm sure it isn't, Stevie would have asked for the money already."

"Let me finish," the chief said, irritated. "Would Stevie know that Katherine would pay the ransom given the fact she and you are such good friends?"

Colleen shook her head in shocked disbelief.

"If Stevie was going to kidnap Mum, why now?" Katherine asked. "He's had plenty of time over the years to abduct her when she was visiting Colleen or me. Why would he commit this alleged crime in a town other than Erie?"

The chief didn't answer and continued, "Did either of you know Mr. Sanders is an ex-con who did time for armed robbery?"

Colleen nodded.

Katherine said, "Yes, I'm aware of that, but Stevie is not the same person he was. He's a responsible father to his daughter, he has a thriving business in Erie, and he's building a good reputation in town. You can ask Chief London about Stevie. I know he'll vouch for him."

"What makes you think I haven't already done that?" The chief stood up and walked to the door. "Thank you, ladies, for coming in on such short notice."

Colleen said, exasperated, "That's it? That's all you have?"

"Meaning?" the chief asked, annoyed.

Colleen apologized, "I'm sorry I was so abrupt, but have you interviewed the person Stevie was with?"

"This is a police matter. I can't discuss who I do or don't interview. I'll be in touch." The chief left the room, then popped her head back in. "Also, I want to make myself perfectly clear. I don't need you two playing amateur sleuths and messing up my investigation."

"How have we done that?" Katherine asked.

"I mean no more canvassing the area, interviewing folks. Let the police handle it. Got it?"

"Yes, we do," Katherine said.

Colleen didn't answer.

"Do you understand, Colleen?"

"Yes, ma'am."

"I noticed your contact info is on the missing person flyer. Have you received any calls with information that could help our investigation?"

"No one has called."

"If someone does call about the case, direct them to the police. Alrighty then. I'll be in touch." The chief left.

Colleen whispered, "Can you text Stevie and ask him what's going on?"

"Come on. Let's get out of here."

Colleen led the way out. She was already out the door when Katherine overheard the chief telling Officer Grant to bring the suspects in.

Katherine hurried out.

Colleen said, "Let's find a place where you can send Stevie a text."

"I'm not sure that's a good idea."

"It's just a text to a friend."

"No, I won't text him."

"Why not?"

"Because the police are on it. I just overheard the chief tell Officer Grant to bring both of the suspects in for questioning."

"Both of them? You mean the guy Stevie was with is a suspect, too?"

"I really don't know, but it makes sense that he is. Wish I had his name."

"Just text Stevie and find out? Or give me his number and I'll text him."

"If I do that, I would be obstructing justice or impeding an official investigation," Katherine replied dramatically.

"It's suspicious that Stevie is here. Did he ever say anything to you about Mum, like he didn't like her or anything negative?"

"No, never. In fact, I don't remember him ever mentioning her name. Let's head back to the café and hope that Holly Martin is still there."

"What do you want with her?" Colleen asked.

"I want to ask her if she was Stevie's server this morning and if she knows the guy he was with."

Colleen smirked. "Wait. Didn't we just tell Chief Merrill we wouldn't canvas the area anymore?"

"I don't see how going into a restaurant and ordering a cup of coffee has anything to do with canvassing."

"You're sly as a fox, Katz."

"More like sly as a cat."

The two walked to Melody Café and waited to be seated. A server came from behind the bar and seated them. Her name tag said Marcie Wagner.

After Marcie took their drink order, Colleen asked, "Is Holly Martin here? We talked to her this morning and wanted to talk to her again."

"Sure. I don't think she's gone home yet. I can go get her. What's this about?"

"I'm the daughter of the woman who is missing."

"Oh, you poor dear. I'll go fetch her for you. Be right back."

The server headed to the back and soon Holly came out to the table. "Marcie said you wanted to talk to me."

"Yes, we very much would appreciate it. Please join us," Colleen said graciously.

"I only have a few minutes. I have to pick my daughter up at daycare." Holly drew up a chair.

Marcie brought a cup of coffee and a cup of tea to the table. She also brought a to-go cup drink for Holly. "Hey, thanks," Holly called after her. "You're a doll."

Marcie smiled and went back to the bar.

Colleen began, "Chief Merrill said she'd talked to you. Thank you so much for telling her what you told us."

"No problem."

"The chief said that while she was here, there were two men she also talked to. Do you remember them?"

"Oh, yes, I was their server. I don't know the name of the guy on the left, but I certainly do the other one," she said negatively.

Katherine leaned in with interest. "Which one do you know? Does he have blond hair?"

"No, the blond-haired guy was nice. I meant that no good bastard John Smith."

Colleen burst out, "Did you say John Smith?"

"Yeah, do you know him?"

"My mother lives in Manhattan and met a John Smith from Melody on an online dating site. She came here to meet him and she's been missing ever since."

"Oh, is that what happened. No one told me this."

Colleen said, "It's on the flyer."

"Yeah, I know, but it didn't say anything about online dating and John Smith. It just said your mom was missing in Melody. I feel so bad for her."

"Oh, yes, you're right. Sorry," Colleen apologized.

Katherine added, "We're not positive that the John Smith in your restaurant is the John Smith who may have kidnapped or harmed Colleen's mother."

"I wouldn't be surprised if he was."

"Why do you say that?" Colleen asked hurriedly.

"Because John's a psycho. Look, I take that back. I shouldn't have said that."

Katherine changed the subject. "When Maggie Murphy came into the café to cash a check, you said you caught a glimpse of the man who was waiting for her outside."

"Not exactly. I said it was dark out and I only saw the back of him."

"Could it have been John Smith?" Colleen asked.

"I can't be certain."

"Let's go back to when you said John was a psycho. What did you mean by that?" Colleen asked nervously.

"I really shouldn't say anything negative about customers. I could get into trouble."

"We won't tell anyone. Promise," Katherine said.

"Let me give you the heads up. He's just out of prison and involved in a work release program. He came in to the café and started hitting on me. He asked me out so many times, I finally said yes. I mean, don't get me wrong, he's good looking. I didn't care if he was a few years older than me."

"So, what happened on your date?" Katherine asked.

"He took me to a bar, ordered me a few drinks, then he said he wanted to take me to where he'd set up a temporary office for the business he was starting."

"What's his line of work?" Katherine asked.

"He's an electrician."

"Okay, did you go there?" Colleen coaxed for more information.

"Like an idiot I did."

"Where was it?"

"I really don't know. I wasn't paying attention when he drove me there, but it was close to the main drag.

It was pouring down rain and I could hardly see out the windshield."

"Then what happened?"

"You'll never believe where his office was?"

"Where?" Colleen and Katherine asked at the same time.

"In a smelly old basement. I should have known better to go down there with him, but sometimes when you drink too much, you do stupid things."

"What happened?" Katherine asked.

"He showed me his storage room full of electrical stuff, then said he'd show me his special room."

Katherine's eyes widened. "Special room," she repeated.

"It had a padded door with a padlock on it. I was totally creeped out, so I insisted that he take me home. He got mad, yanked me by the arm, and pushed me against the door. I put up a fight and got away from him. I ran like hell."

"Did you call the police?"

"No," Holly said adamantly. "The last thing I want to do is call the police when I'm drunk. I've got priors hanging over me. And, please do not repeat what I've said to you to the police."

Colleen said, "Think hard. Where was this place?"

"It was in one of those old houses on Main Street. I can't say which one. To me, they all look the same. You have to remember? It was raining super-hard and I didn't notice my surroundings. I just remember running like the wind to get away from him."

"I assume you did get away from him?" Colleen asked.

"Yep, sure did. I ran back to the café and used my key to get in, then I phoned my friend to come and get me."

Katherine said, "Sounds like the date from hell."

"I'm telling you. The man is certifiably insane."

"You wouldn't happen to know where he lives?" Colleen asked.

"No, I'm sorry. I don't." Holly looked at her watch, "I really have to go."

"Thank you, Holly," Colleen said. "Your secret is safe with us."

As soon as Holly left the building, Colleen said, "A special room in a basement with a padded door waves a big, red flag, don't you think?"

"Let's not leap to conclusions. Maybe it really was his office. Holly got spooked and didn't go in to check it out."

"Would you?" Colleen asked incredulously.

"Heaven's no. I wouldn't have gone down there in the first place."

"Me either."

"I wish Holly would have been sober," Katherine said.

"Why?"

"So, she could give us an address. What should we do? Walk up and down Main Street, stop at every old house and ask the owner if they've seen Mum."

"I don't think that's feasible," Colleen said. "I'd bet most people wouldn't open their doors to strangers. They'd think we were trying to sell them something. And, if you were the guilty party, would you say come on in and look at my basement?"

"Of course not."

"I have a better idea. I'm surprised we haven't thought of this already. Remember the first time we talked to Chief Merrill and she mentioned two John Smiths in town? One was in a convalescent home and the other was a family man."

"Right."

"Let's find out where the family man lives," Colleen said, looking at her phone. "When I called both of them on Monday, I wrote their addresses in my Notes. Hang on. I'll retrieve it." Colleen pulled up the screen, then said, "The John Smith with kids doesn't live on Main Street."

"How do you know it's the John Smith with kids?"

"Process of elimination. The other John Smith lives in a convalescent home."

"Okay, got it. Does the family man live close to Main Street?"

"Hold on. I'll Google it." Colleen punched in the address, then showed Katherine her screen. "That's on the other side of town."

"Darn. If he lived in one of those old homes on Main Street, eureka, we'd have something to go to the chief with."

"You don't think we have something now?" Colleen asked.

"No, not really. I think the chief knows about John Smith, but isn't able to discuss it with us. After all, it's official police business."

"And if Holly knows John Smith is out of prison, I'm betting the chief knows as well."

"Small town. Everyone knows each other's business," Katherine said knowingly.

"Do you think it's possible that Stevie knew John in prison?"

"Maybe, assuming they were in the same prison, but we don't know where John was incarcerated."

"Where was Stevie?" Colleen asked.

"Michigan City."

"That's right. I remember now. I got the impression that the chief was biased against out-of-towners."

"Me, too. She immediately pointed the finger at Stevie and not John."

"There's a word for that. Let me think," Colleen said.

"Small town xenophobia."

"Yep, 'tis it. Should I call the chief and tell her about what Holly said about John?"

"And tell her what? That John was the date from hell and that she was drunk? That his office was in a smelly basement and it had an odd-looking door? No, because all that has nothing to do with Mum being missing."

"Okay, I see your point. Holly was too impaired to be a reliable witness. I don't want to get her into trouble with the law. She was kind enough to tell us she'd seen Mum. She didn't have to do that."

"Exactly, but do you know what really bugs me?"

"No."

"The chief had ample opportunity to tell us the name of the man with Stevie and how he's an ex-con. She called Stevie by his name, but couldn't tell us who Stevie was talking to, especially when we specifically asked about the number of John Smiths in Melody."

"It bugs me too."

Katherine got up from her chair. "Let's get the check and head back to Melody Manor."

"Then what?"

"Wait for the chief to call you if there's more information." Katherine felt around in her jeans' pocket for loose change for the gratuity and pulled out the gold claddagh ring Abra had found. "Oh, Colleen, I almost forgot. Here's your ring."

"What?" Colleen said, surprised, looking at it.

"It's yours, right?"

"No, I'm wearing mine," she said, concerned.

"I guess I should turn it into Mrs. Richards. One of her guests must have lost it. Abra found it in the bathroom."

The color drained from Colleen's face. "No, Katz. I think that's Mum's ring."

Chapter Thirteen

Wednesday Late Afternoon

Chief Merrill parked her police cruiser in the parking lot behind the Melody Manor owned by Sarah Richards and strode up to the side door. She hadn't talked to Sarah since they had a falling out about a parking issue. The owner had three designated spaces behind her B&B and when it was full, she instructed guests to park in the church parking lot next door. The pastor wasn't happy about it and complained. So, when the chief approached Sarah to discuss the problem, Sarah slammed the door in her face.

Today, she wondered how receptive Sarah would be to her asking a few questions. She rang the doorbell several times and when Sarah didn't answer, she tried the doorknob, found it unlocked, and walked in. "Sarah," she called. "It's Chief Merrill. I need to speak to you."

Sarah came down the hall. "What do you want?" she said in an unforgiving tone of not letting bygones be bygones.

"Is John home?"

"My ex-husband John? You know as well as I do that he passed away. You came to the funeral."

"I meant John Jr."

"Whatever do you mean? John doesn't live here."

"This is the address on file with the work release program."

"Oh, that," she said dismissively. "He uses this address for his business, but he lives on the other side of town in the trailer park."

"Could I have his address?"

"Why?"

"I need to talk to him."

"About what?"

"Let's start with you giving me his address."

"Oh, all right. There's no need to be pushy. It's 720 Chesterfield Road, trailer #30. It's a rusted piece of junk. You can't miss it. Now, what do you want with John?"

"Do you know his whereabouts over the weekend?"

"Yeah, why?"

"Where was he?"

"Why don't you ask him yourself?"

The chief grew impatient with Sarah's inability—or unwillingness—to answer simple questions. "Do I have to haul you off to the station to formally ask you a few questions?"

"Well, no. I have a business to run."

"Allow me to repeat my last question. Where was John on Friday night?"

"He was here at the B&B."

"Why? Does John work here?"

"Yes, when I'm out-of-town, John takes care of the Manor."

"You mean take care of the guests? Do you have a register with their names and addresses on it?"

"Why, sure. It's right here," Mrs. Richards said, fumbling through a stack of papers. "Here it is. Friday through check-out Monday morning."

The chief studied the list of names. Not finding what she was looking for, she asked, "Did a Maggie Murphy stay here over the weekend?"

"If her name isn't on the list, then she didn't stay here," Mrs. Richards said with a scowl. "Why does everyone think she stayed here?"

"Who's everyone?"

"Oh, her daughter and her friend. They're staying here right now."

The chief backtracked. "I see three names here, staying in three rooms. I assume married couples."

"Yes. Of course, they're married. What do you think, I'm running a brothel here?"

"How many bedrooms do you rent out?"

"Four," Mrs. Richards answered.

"So, you weren't fully booked over the weekend?"

"No."

"One of your rooms was available?"

"Not really, because John stayed in that room. I couldn't very well have him drive back and forth from that dump he lives in, to tend to my guests. He had to prepare their breakfast. He had to make a good impression. I have a B&B to run. I'm dependent on getting good reviews from my customers to keep up my good standing."

"Online you mean?"

"Why, yes. You don't think I rent to locals, do you?" Mrs. Richards asked with disdain.

The chief ignored the sarcasm. "Is the room John stayed in available for me to look at?"

"Certainly not. I have a guest there. Her name is Katherine Cokenberger. And, she has cats. She's made it perfectly clear no one but her should go into that room."

"Why is that?"

"Because she has two Siamese monsters that got out of her room and tore up my plant room." Mrs. Richards gave the chief a brief account of the escapades of the two escapees, and ended with, "I can't be sure, but I think they ate one of my fish."

The chief cut her off, "Okay, then, I don't need to see the room, and just for the record, I have a Siamese cat. She's the sweetest feline on this planet. Good day, Sarah."

The chief left and received a call from Officer Grant. "Is he at the station?" she asked into the phone. "Good. I'm coming right back."

Hurrying down the sidewalk, the chief bumped into Katherine and Colleen, who had just returned to the B&B.

Colleen asked, "Why are you here?"

"I can't talk now," the chief said, rushing off.

Katherine and Colleen exchanged curious glances. They waited for the chief to drive away, then Colleen asked, "What was that all about? She ran out of here like it was a house on fire."

"If she hadn't been in such a hurry, I would have mentioned Mum's ring."

"Those rings are a dime a dozen," Colleen said, dejected. "I bet there are millions of women out there who wear them. I can't say for sure it belongs to Mum."

"Really?"

"Yes, really. When you go on a tour of Ireland, you can buy them at the tourist souvenirs shops. I've seen them here in jewelry stores."

"If the ring belongs to Mum, then that would prove where she was staying," Katherine said, still trying to convince Colleen that they should tell the chief.

"Katz, you said that Abra was playing with it. She probably found it yesterday when the two of them went fishing. I can see her right now, clamping down on it with her dainty little jaw."

Mrs. Richards stormed out of the house, clutching her handbag close to her chest. She passed them on the sidewalk and didn't offer a greeting. She hurried to her Mercedes, started the engine, and took off like a bat out of hell.

"Whoa," Katherine said. "Somebody isn't happy."

"Does this mean we have the place to ourselves?"

"Kind of looks like it, but I don't know for how long." Katherine grabbed her cellphone and asked, "Can you give me Chief Merrill's number?"

"Why?"

"I'm reporting the ring. I found it. I should be the one to tell the chief."

Colleen took her phone out of her purse and scrolled through her contacts list. "Here it is," she said, showing Katherine her phone.

Katherine punched in the number and called the chief. The call went to voicemail. She left a brief message about the discovery of the ring and how she thought it belonged to Mum. She finished the call by saying she believed Mum had stayed in the room over the weekend, and for reasons unknown, she'd vacated it before Colleen and she had arrived. She suspected that Mrs. Richards knew this and was withholding critical information.

Colleen put her phone back and observed, "Well said, Katz. Let's just hope the chief listens to her voicemail soon and comes back to talk to Mrs. Richards. I'm sorry I didn't see the connection like you did."

"It's circumstantial at best. But you can't say I didn't try."

Colleen sat down on one of the patio chairs. "Katz, I've been thinking. We don't need to stay here tonight."

"What do you mean?"

"There's nothing else left for us to do. If Chief Merrill finds out anything, she'll call. Can we drive home tonight?"

"I'm game, if you do some of the driving. I'm still tired from not getting any sleep."

Colleen bounced out of her chair. "Let's go pack while Mrs. Richards is gone. Then we can tell her we're leaving, when we're *actually* leaving."

"Makes sense. Let's pack your stuff first and put it in the Outback."

"Great, then we'll go upstairs, get your stuff, load up the cats, and take off. We can stop somewhere near Indy to eat like at a McDonald's or Arby's."

"Perfect. If Mrs. Richards isn't back, I'll write her a note," Katherine said.

"No, I'll do it. I made the reservation. Hey, what time is it? I'm too lazy to check my phone."

"It's a quarter till five."

"So, we can probably be on the road by six?"

"Maybe before then."

Katherine held open the side door and Colleen stepped in. She walked to her room and Katherine followed.

Chapter Fourteen

Back at the Station

Stevie sat on an uncomfortable wood chair in the interview room of the Melody police. He'd been taking a nap in his truck when a police officer walked up and tapped on his window, waking him up. The officer said he was a person of interest in an ongoing missing person case, and when Stevie protested, the officer said he had to go to the station and talk with Chief Merrill.

Stevie, well aware of police procedure, did not argue with the man and said he'd come willingly, but he would follow the officer to the station. He didn't want to leave his truck in a near-empty parking lot. The officer said no, he would have to ride with him.

Stevie suspected the officer probably thought he was a flight risk or he was going to get him down at the station, arrest him and throw him in jail. The latter worried him because there was no way he could get in touch with Rachael to explain to her what was going on. He could have kicked himself for not getting her address when he saw her, in case something did go wrong, like his truck conking out again. But there wasn't time for that. She seemed to be in a genuine hurry to get him out of the restaurant before anyone else saw him.

Stevie nervously drummed his fingers on the table and waited impatiently for someone to show up and start the show. He'd been in these kind of rooms on several occasions and knew what to expect. He surmised that the chief would come in with another officer. She'd play the good cop and the other would come after him like a ravenous badger. He glanced at his watch for the millionth time and saw that it was four-thirty. He was more nervous about standing Rachael up than his own predicament.

He thought that he'd screwed up by not calling the chief and telling her his suspicions about Smitty. He was afraid she'd want to talk in person and he'd miss his rendezvous. So, here he was at the station anyway and it looked like he'd be there for a while.

After fifteen minutes had gone by, the chief popped her head in the door and said in a friendly voice, "You want a soda pop or a coffee? We have one of those Keurig machines with different flavored pods."

"No, thank you," Stevie said, then lowered his voice, "How about an interrogation pod?"

"Come again?" the chief asked.

"No, I'm good."

"Okay, then," she said, walking in. She closed the door behind her. "I'm sorry for your wait."

"No problem," Stevie said. He was relieved it was just the chief and no one else. He prayed that the interview wouldn't take much time and that he'd be on his way.

The chief sat across from Stevie, set down a file folder and opened her iPad. "Let's first talk about Maggie Murphy." She took the missing person flyer out of the folder and slid it across the table. "Back at the café you said you knew her because she was Katherine Cokenberger's best friend's mother?"

"Yes."

"Did you have feelings for Colleen?"

"What kind of feelings?"

"Of the amorous kind. Did her mother not approve and stood in the way of you two hooking up?"

"Stood in the way?" Stevie asked. "How?"

"Like she didn't approve of you seeing Colleen because you're an ex-con?" the chief asked suspiciously.

"I don't know Maggie or Colleen on a personal basis. What I do know about the two of them has been through my friend, Katz."

"How often have you seen Maggie, say over the past few years?"

"A few times. She rarely comes to town because she lives in Manhattan."

"Okay, what do you know about her?"

"I know that whenever she visits Katz, she does stupid things."

"You're calling her stupid?"

"I'm not calling her stupid, but some of the brainless things she does puts other people's lives at stake."

"Give me an example?"

"A few years ago, Maggie Murphy stayed with Katz at the pink mansion—"

"Pink mansion?" the chief interrupted.

"Katz lives in her late great aunt's Victorian mansion. It's in one of Erie's historic districts. It's painted pink."

"Oh, okay, go on."

"There was an escaped prisoner gunning for Katherine and when Katz left the house, she told Maggie to not disarm the security system and let anyone in. Maggie did exactly the opposite of what Katz said to do. She let in a criminal who shot Jake."

"Jake?"

"Katz's husband, although they were not married at the time of the shooting."

"When was the last time you saw Maggie Murphy in Erie?"

"I saw her last spring, but it wasn't in Erie. It was in Seagull, Indiana."

"Seagull's up north by the Indiana Dunes?"

"Yes. I had a date with a woman renting a cabin next to the cabin Katz, Colleen and Maggie were sharing. I didn't talk to her, I just heard about her. Katz was upset because Maggie tried to light a water heater and caught the cabin on fire. When the firemen put out the fire, Katz's cats got outside. She was very upset because the Siamese are indoor only."

"What are the chances of you dating a woman staying next to people you know from Erie?"

"That's what I thought."

The chief opened her folder again and pulled out a printed sheet. "I had one of my officer's run a check on you. You have quite a history."

Stevie was quiet and didn't comment.

"You were sent to prison for armed robbery. Served your time. One of your known associates is your late father, Sam Sanders, is that correct?"

"Yes."

"Sam Sanders was the alleged crime boss of a large portion of this state, involved in drug trafficking, manufacturing meth and angel dust, running houses of ill repute, but he never served time for these crimes."

"Everything you just said is true."

"I also learned that your father was gunned down by a deputy from Brook County."

"Yes." Stevie didn't care to elaborate.

"The shooting occurred at a residence Katherine Cokenberger was renting."

"Yes. Katz and Jake rented a farmhouse while their home was being remodeled."

"And, Maggie Murphy's daughter was there?"

"Colleen was there."

"Both these parties were at the residence when Deputy Daryl Cokenberger shot your father?"

"Yes."

"And, you were there?"

"Yes, as well as other people."

"What were you doing there?"

"My daughter woke up in the middle of the night screaming that something bad was going to happen to Katz. She was so upset, I called Jake, he came and got us and the three of us went to the farmhouse."

"Is it common for your daughter to wake up and make predictions about people?"

"No, just this one time. Salina and Katz are very close. She was worried that Katz and Colleen were at the house by themselves because Daryl and Jake were driving somewhere out-of-state to a car show. Daryl is an old car enthusiast."

"Why would she be afraid of two grown women staying alone in a, what did you call it, farmhouse?"

"I don't know. Katz was nervous about staying in the house alone, so Colleen volunteered to stay with her."

"Why would she be afraid?"

"Because she'd just moved into it. I don't know."

"Where was this house?"

"In the country."

"So, the way I look at it, Colleen's husband, Daryl, shot your father. Did you kidnap or cause harm to Colleen's mother out of revenge for the death of your father?" The chief moved forward in her chair to read Stevie's facial expression.

"Chief, I must be honest with you. I loved my father, but I didn't condone his criminal activities. Daryl, I mean, Deputy Cokenberger, shot my father because he had a gun aimed at Katz."

The chief sat back in her chair. She realized she wasn't getting anywhere with her line of questioning. She changed the subject, "Let's talk about John Smith. How do you know him?"

"We served time at the penitentiary in Michigan City. Smitty was working in an electrical shop the same time I was. We struck up a friendship."

"It must have been a strong friendship to keep in touch all of these years, since you were released several years before he was."

"Actually, he just recently reached out to me. He friended me on Facebook, then we starting emailing each other. Smitty was picking my brain about starting an electric contracting business in Melody."

"And that's the reason why you drove three hours to meet up with him, to talk about his business plans?"

"That pretty much sums it up," Stevie said, hoping the chief wouldn't ask him if there was another reason.

"I learned that you were supposed to be in Chicago for a trade show. Yet, here you are. How do you explain that?"

"Yes, I'm supposed to be in Chicago, but not until tomorrow. The show runs from Thursday through Saturday. Since my daughter is out-of-town on a class trip this week, I thought I'd take a little personal time and take a long drive to help an old friend."

"What were John and you talking about during breakfast this morning?"

"Basically, we talked about Smitty renting a storefront where he could hang his shingle. I suggested one of the shops on Main Street. I also said he needed to buy a newer pickup so he could have his company's logo painted on it."

"When I was talking to the gal at the bar, I looked over at your table, and it looked like you were discussing something other than the electric business. You looked like you disapproved of something John had said. It would really help my case, if you'd let me know what it was."

"I think Smitty doesn't treat women very well."

"Why do you think that?"

"He's a womanizer and takes women out for one-night-stands."

"Did he mention any names of women he'd taken out?"

"Yeah, he said he had a date with the gal who served our table."

"The gal I was talking to at the bar? Holly Martin?"

Stevie nodded. "She disliked Smitty so much she wouldn't even look at him. When Smitty asked her why, she said she wouldn't repeat what he'd done to her in mixed company."

"Did she say what she meant by that?"

"No, she didn't."

"Um, did he mention anyone else?"

"Yes, he did. And, that's what I was meaning to call you about, but I fell asleep in my truck." Stevie absent-mindedly looked at his watch.

"Okay, what is it you wanted to tell me?"

"Smitty said he had a date with an older woman on Saturday night. He'd met her on an online dating site and picked her up at the airport in Louisville. He said he took her to Rusty's Roadhouse. They didn't get along, so he dumped her."

"Dumped her?"

"That's what I wanted to ask about, but I think he was on to me for asking too many questions. I think Smitty knows the whereabouts of Maggie." Stevie didn't volunteer that he thought Smitty was dangerous and might have harmed her.

The chief asked, "Would you be prepared to write a witness statement and sign it for me?"

"Well, yes, but I can't do it now."

"I notice you looked at your watch. Do you need to be somewhere?"

Stevie thought fast on his feet. "I need to drive to Chicago. It's about a five-hour drive from here, so I really want to get started."

"I'm sorry but I have to delay you. I need your statement in order to issue a warrant for John Smith's arrest."

Stevie felt both relieved that Smitty was going to be arrested and that he might confess to where Maggie was. But he also felt crushed. He didn't know how long this statement process would take, but it certainly would be past five o'clock when he planned on picking up Rachael.

The chief read his mind. "I tell you what. I'll get someone in here right now to take the dictation. She'll print it and you'll sign it. Then, you can be on your way. How does that sound?"

"Perfect," he said, faking a smile. "Thank you," he said as she left the room.

Chapter Fifteen

Rusty's Roadhouse

Rachael glanced at the clock and realized it was five o'clock, so she hurriedly took off her apron and headed out the restaurant's back door. She noticed a beat-up pickup parked outside. When she walked by and looked in, she was surprised to see a man sitting behind the steering wheel, but then thought that maybe he was picking up someone. She'd never seen that truck before. She thought she'd recognized the man but couldn't remember when or where she'd seen him. When he smiled and waved, she ignored him and made her way to the highway.

There wasn't a sidewalk, so she carefully walked on the narrow shoulder and avoided falling into the deep concrete drainage ditch running next to it. She'd wondered why she picked today to not drive her car, but she hadn't expected to ever see Stevie again. She hadn't walked more than a few feet when the driver of the pickup started his vehicle and pulled out. He drove slowly behind her. Rachael flinched and wondered what the man could want. She immediately thought of the mob, but knew that no mobster she'd ever known would drive such a battered vehicle. She took a deep breath and speculated that the man was someone she'd served at the restaurant. She thought, *He wouldn't be the first to have a crush on me, but I've never had anyone follow me. This is freaking me out.*

The driver sped up in front of her, parked at a diagonal, and got out. "Hey, Rachael," he called, rushing over to her. "I've got a message from Stevie."

Rachael had nowhere to run except to turn around and head back to the restaurant, but he was already right next to her. "Why did you call me Rachael?" she asked. Then it dawned on her that she *had* seen this man before. He was the one that came into the roadhouse and called her by her former name. "You have me mixed up with someone else. My name is Sally. If you'll excuse me, I'm trying to walk here." She prayed someone would drive by and the man would have to move his truck and be on his way. She prayed that someone would be Stevie.

"My name is Smitty. I'm a friend of Stevie's. I had breakfast with him this morning. He just called me and said his truck broke down and he wanted me to take you to him. He's at the Melody car dealership. You know, the one on the other side of town?" he lied.

Smitty was proud of his ability to lie at the spur of the moment. Stevie told him he had truck trouble the night before and had to spend the night in Scottsburg, waiting for a part. As an ex-con, Smitty knew that if he was going to lie, he'd better incorporate a little bit of the truth in it. That way, if he got caught, he'd remember the true parts of the lie and wriggle his way out of it. When he happened to drive by the police station and see Officer Grant escort Stevie inside, he knew his friend had turned traitor and was reporting him. He really screwed up when he told Stevie about the date with the older woman he met online. He was furious. He couldn't believe that he trusted this guy.

Smitty also had a gift to put two and two together, almost a psychic sense. He thought Stevie wasn't a convincing liar when he said the woman at the roadhouse wasn't Rachael. He knew he was lying. Hell, she looked just like the picture Stevie had emailed to him. He was angry at Stevie and had to find a way to get back at him. He had to figure out how he'd get to Rachael, so he could hurt her and give Stevie a dose of his own medicine. And it turned out to be super-easy to track her down. He called the roadhouse, asked for Sally, and when the person on the other end said he'd go get her, he knew Rachael was working today and that the servers changed shifts at five o'clock. He found the perfect parking spot, right next to the back door, and he waited for her to come out. Easy-peasy.

"I don't know anyone named Stevie," Rachael said anxiously, wondering how she was going to get out of this situation. She could jump in the ditch, but would probably break an ankle. She could put up a fight, but she knew her small frame couldn't compete with Smitty, who could easily overpower her. "Now get the hell out of my way," she demanded, shoving past Smitty.

Smitty grabbed her by the arm and pulled her into a chokehold. Rachael brought her knees up and began digging her heels in his shins. She pinched the insides of his arms. Smitty lost balance and fell against the truck. When he released her, Rachael escaped and started to run back toward the restaurant.

Ashley was driving home and saw the truck parked at a weird angle close to the side of the road. She stopped behind it, honked her horn and screamed out the window, "What's the matter with you? Get that piece of junk off the highway." Then she noticed Rachael.

Rachael, seeing her friend, ran to the Cherokee, opened the door and climbed in. Smitty yanked Rachael partially out of the vehicle. Rachael held on to the glovebox handle.

"Duck," Ashley said to Rachael, raising a heavy wrench. She smacked Smitty on the head with it. Rachael kicked him out of the way and shut the door. Smitty stumbled into the ditch.

Ashley stepped on the accelerator, sped off, leaving tire marks behind her. "Oh, my god, girl. What's going on?"

"That guy is crazy and forcibly tried to pick me up."

Ashley drove at top speed, not speaking for a few seconds, then asked angrily, "Do you know who that guy is?"

"He said his name was Smitty. He came into the restaurant several nights ago."

"Smitty, huh? And he came into the roadhouse?"

"Yeah, why?"

"Was he with another woman?"

"An older woman, yes."

"How old?"

"She probably was in her sixties."

"Too young to be his mother."

"What's up? Sounds like you know him?"

"That's John Smith. He was my date for Friday night, but right now, I wouldn't go out with him if he paid me a million dollars. Do you want to report him to the police?"

Rachael said hurriedly, "No, I don't want the police involved. I think I hurt him more than he hurt me."

"Gosh, don't forget me? I smacked him with my persuader."

"What's a persuader?"

"My humongous wrench. I always keep it in my Cherokee, just in case."

"I'm glad you do."

"Are you sure we shouldn't report this to the police? What if I injured him? He could go to the police first. I can turn around and drive to the station right now."

"If you want to report it, please do, but I don't want to go to the station right this minute."

"Sure. No problem."

"Oh, you didn't hurt him. I saw him fall in the ditch and then struggle to get out. He's not following us, is he?"

Rachael asked, suddenly terrified Smitty would chase her down.

Ashley checked her mirror. "Nope, don't see him."

"All right. If it's okay, I just want to go home."

"That's where I'm takin' you. I know it's none of my business, but who was that Stevie guy who came into the restaurant this morning? I've been dying to ask you, but we've been so dang busy, I didn't get the chance."

Rachael was momentarily at a loss for words. She didn't want to answer the question, but she knew she had to. She owed it to her friend who had just saved her from whatever the hell that guy was going to do to her. "He's someone I used to know. The other day, he was passing through town and thought he'd seen me walk into the roadhouse, but he couldn't stop because he had to be somewhere, but the next time he came to town, he stopped to check it out."

"This morning, you mean?"

"Yes, I really like him a lot and we were to meet up." Rachael's voice trailed off as she paused to think of something plausible to say that wasn't a down-and-out lie to her friend. "We were going to meet up later."

"Oh, okay, and Miss Sally, you don't have to walk home after working a busy shift. Those days you don't drive, I would gladly pick you up and take you home. Girl, I just live down the road."

"Thanks, Ashley. That's very sweet of you. But, if you would have driven me home today, I would have missed out on all that drama back there," she joked, trying to make light out of something scary that had just happened.

Ashley didn't think it was funny. "If I hadn't of come along, he could have hurt you."

"Nah, I don't think so. Let's just forget it. Hey, can you drop me off at the community mailboxes? I want to get my mail. I can walk the rest of the way to my apartment."

"Sure, no problem," Ashley said, driving in.

Rachael got out and said, "Thanks for the lift."

"Any time! See you tomorrow."

"Yep," Rachael said, waving.

After Ashley had pulled back on the highway, Rachael didn't check to see if she'd received any mail, she walked directly to her car. She worried about why Stevie hadn't picked her up. Looking at her watch, she saw that it was half past five, so she got in her car and drove to town, looking for Stevie's red Dodge Ram.

She drove down countless streets off the main drag, then searched parking lots. She was just about to give up, when she spotted Stevie's truck. She pulled up behind it, observed the license plates had an Erie County number on them, and parked next to it. She'd wait in her vehicle until he came back. She wondered where he was and why he'd missed the rendezvous time. Then, she realized that Smitty's story about Stevie's car being at the dealership was a blatant lie, but why would Smitty say Stevie told him to pick her up? What was their connection?

After waiting for a half hour, Rachael looked in her side-view mirror and saw Stevie walking through the parking lot. She climbed out of her car.

When he saw her, he ran and grabbed her, twirling her around. "I'm so glad to see you, but listen, we have to get out of here. I'll explain in the truck."

While Rachael was retrieving her purse out of her car and locking the doors, Stevie opened the truck's passenger door for her. She grabbed the overhead bar and climbed in. Stevie raced to the other side, got in and quickly fired up the engine. He drove out of the parking lot and straight to the highway that led to the interstate.

Rachael was very quiet. Stevie reached over and took her hand. "We have a lot to talk about."

She answered, "Yes, we do, but first, I must ask, did you come to Melody to look for me or did you come to meet up with your friend, Smitty?"

"How do you know about him?"

"He just tried to pick me up while I was walking home from work. He said you told him to give me a ride. Is that true?"

"That lying piece of crap," Stevie said, pounding his fist on the steering wheel. "Did he hurt you?"

"No, but he scared the hell out of me. If it hadn't been for my friend Ashley, who knows what he would have done to me?"

Stevie said, "It's a long story, but I can explain what I know and how I know. Is it okay if you and I take a little drive?"

"Yes, of course. I have some major things to talk to you about, too."

"Good. Is it okay if you leave your car in the parking lot?"

"Sure. No problem. I don't think anyone would want to steal an ancient Mazda. Besides, what criminal would attempt to do that when the parking lot is so close to the police station?"

Stevie laughed. "Good point. Can you call your boss and tell him or her you're taking a few days off?"

"I can, but he might be suspicious about why I want the time off."

"Explain to him that something came up and you have personal business to attend to."

"Okay, I'll do that, but I'll have to buy a burner phone."

"You don't have a cell?"

"Nope. Back in my apartment, I have an old-fashioned landline."

"Okay, we'll find a store that sells them. Will you get into trouble with the Feds if I take you to a place outside of Melody? It's off the beaten track."

"No, I'm not required to get their permission to do anything, but where are you taking me?"

"Last month, I closed on a real estate deal. I bought two hundred wooded acres. On this property, there's a two-thousand-square foot, double-story cabin. It's set back from the road. It was in move-in-ready condition but I've changed the wiring, bought new kitchen appliances, and painted a few of the rooms."

"You're taking me to Erie?" Rachael asked, surprised, not commenting on the cabin.

"No, not to the town, but in the country. The cabin is several miles from Chester's Kiosk—the best BBQ this side of the Mississippi. You remember, don't you?"

Rachael didn't answer.

"Trust me, it's really out in the country. I'll use the back roads to get there. No one will see us. We can be together, so we can talk things out."

"What about Salina?"

"Salina's away this week on a class trip."

"Did you say you bought a cabin? To live in or to rent?"

"To live in."

"Won't Salina be upset that you're moving when she's so attached to living next door to Katz?"

"Probably, but she'll have to get over it. She'll be upset at first, but it's not like we're moving to another state. I'm buying her a car for her graduation present; she can drive over to see Katz anytime she wants too. Besides,

Salina is going off to college this summer. Before my father died, he set up a sizeable trust for her to go."

"What about your house in Erie?"

"I'm selling my house."

"Oh, Stevie, pull over. I want to kiss you so much; I can't stand it any longer."

"Yes, ma'am," he said, finding a place to park. He gathered Rachael in his arms and kissed her tenderly.

She held onto him and whispered, "I have missed you so much. I haven't once stopped thinking about you."

Stevie pushed a strand of her long, blond hair away from her face. "I've missed you more." He hugged her for a long time, kissed her on the forehead and said, "It's a good three-hour drive to Erie, so we better get started. We can stop in Scottsburg and eat dinner, then head up north?"

"How about we grab a burger and eat on the way?" she suggested.

"Sounds good."

"Can you find a barbecue place like Chester's? I'll have the mild sauce on my sandwich with chips instead of fries."

Stevie laughed, then drove back onto the highway. "You did remember." His eyes twinkled when he thought back on that hot day in July when he took Rachael to Chester's kiosk across from his wind turbine farm.

"How can I forget? Technically, it was our first date."

"It was the perfect date."

"I'm sure we'll have more of them."

"You bet. Now, it's a good hour's drive to Scottsburg, so why don't you tell me what you've been up to these past few months?"

Rachael said, "Oh, we can talk about me later. How about you go first? I'm curious about your connection with John Smith."

"I know him as Smitty." Stevie began filling in Rachael on the details of who, what, when, and why. He ended with his interview by the Melody police chief regarding a missing person—coincidentally the mother of Colleen Cokenberger, Katz's best friend.

"That's more than a coincidence. I hope the police find her and that she's okay."

"The chief had me sign a witness statement about what Smitty told me—that he'd had a date with an older woman he met online and had picked her up at the

Louisville Airport. My hunch is that woman was Maggie Murphy, Colleen's mother."

"Wait. Back up. When did John Smith, Smitty, whoever, have a date with a woman he met online?"

"Last Saturday night. He said they had dinner at the place where you work."

"Oh, this is getting stranger by the second."

"Why?"

"Because I was their server. John Smith came in the restaurant with an attractive woman in her sixties. She had red hair, cut very short, and beautiful green eyes. She looked like she had a lot of class, by the way she was dressed and carried herself. When John called me my real name, I totally freaked out, went to the back and found another server to take care of them."

Stevie opened the center console and pulled out the missing person flyer. "Is this the woman you saw?"

Rachael studied the picture. "Yes, that's her. Should I talk to the police?"

"Might not be a bad idea. You need to talk to Chief Merrill specifically and tell her the name of the server who replaced you."

Rachael didn't say anything.

"But it's probably not necessary."

"Why? I'm confused."

"Because the last thing the chief said to me was that she was issuing a warrant for Smitty's arrest. I spoke to her about how Smitty had taken his date to the roadhouse. She's probably there right now interviewing the staff."

"Okay, then."

"Okay, what?"

"If the police need my two cents, they know where to find me to ask. Right at this moment, I don't want to call attention to myself."

"Understood."

"I pray he doesn't make bail."

"Why?"

"Because if he's off the street, I won't have to worry about him trying to pick me up again. And, my friend Ashley won't have to worry about getting into trouble for hitting him in the head with a wrench."

"What?" Stevie asked, surprised. "Earlier you left out that part."

"Smitty was trying to pull me out of Ashley's car and she hit him."

"Serves him right," Stevie said. "I'm so thankful Ashley came to your rescue when she did."

"My friend is quite a character and I love her dearly."

"Oh, I almost forgot to mention, Katz and Colleen are here in Melody right this very minute."

"For real? Did you talk to them?"

"No, I didn't want to be in the mix of it. Besides, I didn't want anything to prevent me from picking you up at five."

"I'm glad it worked out for us. As much as I think John Smith, Smitty, is a jerk, I'm thankful he called you when he saw me at the roadhouse. It was a miracle."

"I guess that's right."

"But, Stevie, I want you to understand something. I was coming back to you."

"How's that possible?"

"This morning I sent several faxes. One was to my late grandmother's attorney and a second one was to her bank."

"I'm sorry for your loss. I know how close you were to her," Stevie consoled. "I wish I could have met her."

"She would have liked you. Her name was Pearl, but to me she'll aways be my Grammy. She lived in a huge, brick Victorian mansion along the Hudson in Nyack, New York. When I worked for a magician who was performing in the Catskills, my job was to mind two stunningly beautiful and smart Siamese. On the weekends, I'd take them to my Grammy's house. They loved it."

"Scout and Abra, right?"

"Yes, but when I saw them a few months ago the smaller one, Abra, was very stressed. I'd love to see them again, if that's possible."

"Anything is possible," Stevie said.

"I think of my Grammy every day."

"When you think about her, that will help you ease the pain, and when you talk to other people about her, especially to me, that will help also."

"Thank you. You're very kind. What I'm trying to say is my Grammy left me her estate."

"The Victorian house in Nyack?"

"No, she sold the house before she passed. She gave me the proceeds from that sale, except for the furnishings she had auctioned. She gave those to her boyfriend, Lawrence. It's a lot of money. In order to claim it, I had to sign an affidavit using my legal name."

"And, not your alias?"

"Right. I sent three faxes yesterday."

"Do you mind if I ask who the third fax was to?"

"No, I don't mind at all because that fax has an impact on you as well."

"What? How?"

"The last fax I sent was to my handler at the Witness Protection Program. I said thank you very much for what you've done for me but I want my old life back."

"You're leaving the program?" Stevie asked, happily, then added, concerned, "Is it safe for you to do that?"

"Thanks to my testimony, the key principals of the mob are in prison."

"Including Ray Russo?"

"Ray committed suicide in his cell."

Stevie said, shocked, "I never saw that coming."

"I didn't either. I feel I can safely go back to the way things were. I can be Rachael again. In this digital age we live in, the stakes keep getting higher and higher for money-laundering schemes to rake in hundreds of millions of dollars. It's a feeding frenzy for organized crime. I just read in the paper about a bust in New York City. It was the same type of crime Ray was involved in, but different people and for tons of more money."

"Where do you plan to live?"

"Erie."

"Can you move now?"

"I have a few things to finish in Melody. I'm sure the program will have me fill out stuff."

"I would feel a lot better if you'd stay with me. I can protect you. I mean, I've been going crazy worrying about you and wondering if you were okay. No one is going to hurt you while I'm around."

Rachael reached over and squeezed his arm. "I know. That's why I care for you so much."

"How long do you think you'll stay in Melody?"

"Two weeks, max. I have to give my notice at the roadhouse, notify my handler that I'm giving up my studio apartment, and break the news gently to Ashley. If it's sooner, you'll be the first to know."

"How about I stay with you those two weeks? I can cook, clean the apartment, and keep you warm at night."

"I like that idea, but you have your business to run. And, I need to find somewhere to live close to you."

"I didn't sell your storefront."

"You didn't? Did you rent it to any one?"

"Nope."

Rachael was noticeably relieved.

"I made some changes though. I installed a state-of-the-art security system. And I reconfigured your back patio area so a person could park their car and not have nosy neighbors watching their every move."

Rachael spit out a laugh. "You mean that nosy woman across the street? I forget her name."

"Gladys Kramer."

"Oh, I think she's good for the neighborhood as long as she stays out of my business."

"Would you mind living there after the two cops were shot?"

"I wouldn't if either one of them had died. I'm kind of superstitious that way, but since they're okay, I don't think the place would have any bad vibes."

"It doesn't. Oh, and I left everything just like it was when you left. Your clothes are there, so you'll have something to wear. One thing I did do, I cleaned out the refrigerator." Stevie gave a wry smile.

"I'm glad you did," she laughed. "I can only stay until Sunday morning."

"That works. I pick up Salina around five, so that gives me time to drive you back and then meet her bus at the school."

"That's a lot of driving. Why don't you take me back Saturday, we'll have dinner at a nice restaurant, then you can stay overnight with me?"

"That sounds like a great idea, but I have a better plan for the next three days."

"What's that?"

"We can stay at the cabin. I have a guest room that has your name on it."

Rachael considered it for a moment, then said, "I like that idea. No one will see me. Technically, I'm still with the program, so I don't want anyone gossiping about me."

"Yes, ma'am. I can absolutely guarantee that none of the town gossips will see you."

Chapter Sixteen

Back at Melody Manor
What's Going On?

Katherine opened the rear hatch of the Outback and strategically arranged Colleen's suitcase and cosmetic case on one side of the trunk, leaving an open space on the right for her overnight bag and the cat's belongings.

Colleen observed, "Katz, you are a marvel at packing a vehicle."

"Takes practice," Katherine laughed. "Are you sure we got everything out of your room?"

"Sure did."

"Where's your bag with the pajamas in it?"

"Oh, I put it in my suitcase."

"In that case, let's head to my room." Katherine lowered the hatch.

"Sure."

They walked to the side door of Melody Manor.

"We're lucky Mrs. Richards hasn't come back yet," Katherine said, opening the door.

"Why?"

"So, she wouldn't whip out her rules book and quote some infraction we've committed for checking out early."

"She's already charged my credit card for the full amount, so what more does she want?"

Katherine glanced at her watch. "Okay, it shouldn't take long to pack up my stuff, load the cats in the carrier, and take off."

Colleen reflected. "I really miss Daryl."

"I bet you do. I miss Jake and my other cats, too."

They both went inside and headed to the front of the house to the stairs. "Wait, Katz, I have to turn a light on. It's so dark, I can hardly see where I'm going."

"Good luck. None of the lamps have working bulbs in them. Don't waste your time. Just be careful. Take one step at a time."

As the two walked down the upstairs long hallway, Katherine stopped. "Look," she pointed. "My door's standing wide open."

"And someone threw your security wedge in the corner," Colleen said nervously.

"Shhh, the lights have been turned off," Katherine whispered. "It's pitch black in there. Grab your cell and turn on the flashlight. Walk behind me." Katherine slowly approached the room. The hair on the back of her neck rose. She was terrified of what she might find inside.

Slowly entering the room, Katherine flicked the switch to the overhead light. She scanned the room for an intruder. She didn't see anyone or the cats. "Scout. Abra. Come here?"

Colleen said in a frightened voice, "The bathroom door is open. Didn't you say you closed it?"

"Dang, Scout must have opened the door." She rushed in, turned on the light, and panicked when she saw the panel to the pipe chase standing wide open. The turn buttons had been forcibly wrenched out and lay nearby on the floor. A trail of blood droplets led to the opening.

"Oh, the saints preserve us," Colleen said. "Whose blood is that?"

Katherine removed her cell, got down on all fours and flashed the light in the gaping hole. She didn't see anything but ripped foam insulation dangling from the pipes. "The cats are somewhere in this pipe chase."

"They're in there?" Colleen asked, horrified.

"I think so. From the look of the insulation, they climbed down because there isn't any damage up above. We need to find out where these pipes go to."

"Katz, maybe they're not in there. Maybe they went out the open door."

"That's possible, but we need to find them." Katherine grabbed the cat carrier and headed out of the room.

"Where do we start?"

"You look up here. Then go downstairs to the front of the house. In the parlor, check behind the curtains to see if they're sitting on the windowsill. Look underneath every piece of furniture. I'll check the rest of the first floor."

Colleen remained in the room and looked under the bed, while Katherine made her way to the stairs. She hurried down them. She first checked the plant room and prayed the cats were in there. The cats were nowhere in sight. She ran back to the kitchen and set the carrier on the counter, then she searched everywhere, including the cabinet underneath the sink. No Siamese. She moved to Colleen's room and looked underneath the bed. No cats.

Colleen jogged back. "I've looked everywhere. Where can they be?"

"Scout. Abra. Where are you?" Katherine's voice broke.

"Katz, we need to look outside. I have a terrible feeling they got out. Maybe that daft Mrs. Richards let them out."

"I pray they're not out there. The traffic out front is super-busy. I can't even think about them being hit by one of those semi-trucks that whiz by every minute." Katherine grabbed the carrier and the two ran out the door. They raced down the brick sidewalk to the street. Scanning up and down Main Street, they were relieved they didn't see an unthinkable scene.

Heading back to the B&B and walking down the sidewalk, Colleen grabbed Katz by the arm. "Look!" she said, aghast, pointing at one of the basement windows.

Katherine turned and looked. Scout and Abra sat on the windowsill inside the house. "Girls, stay put. I'm coming. Don't move."

When the Siamese saw Katherine and Colleen, they started swaying back and forth. Abra's pupils widened and Scout shrieked a morbid-sounding wail that was muffled by the window glass.

"What are we going to do?" Colleen asked. "The exterior basement doors are locked."

Katherine set the cat carrier down. "Yeah, with a flimsy padlock made last century. I'll get a hammer and smash it open."

"Are you sure that'll work?"

"It does on TV," Katherine said, sprinting to her SUV.

Through the basement window, Colleen tapped on the glass and talked softly to the cats, trying to calm them down. Scout continued shrieking like a banshee; Abra began foaming at the mouth. The cats jumped down and disappeared in the dark void.

Colleen called to the cats, "Oh, no . . . no . . . no. Come back."

Katherine sensed danger. She couldn't explain it, but intuitively she knew she shouldn't go down into the basement without a weapon. She remembered how she'd found her ex-fiancé dead in the basement of the pink mansion. And, a few years later, how the judge who married Jake and her was found murdered in the same basement. She unlocked the Outback's glove box and removed her Glock. She inserted a ten-round magazine, then tucked the gun in the back of her jeans.

Hurrying back to the trunk area, she grabbed a hammer from her toolbox, and headed back to the basement doors. She began pounding the shackle of the padlock. She hit it several times before the lock sprung open. She struggled to lift one of the heavy wood doors.

Colleen stooped down to help her. Once the doors were both open, Colleen cautioned, "Something isn't right. I feel it. We should call the police."

"I'm not leaving my cats down there for one more second." Katherine cautiously went down the stairs one step at a time. "Colleen, hang back, these steps are treacherous."

"I'm not letting you go down there by yourself," Colleen answered stubbornly.

Immediately the two were confronted by a foul smell.

"Oh, what is that?" Colleen asked, covering her nose.

Katherine didn't answer. She extracted her cell and turned on the flashlight. Shining the light into the dark basement, she searched for the Siamese. She held her breath and listened for any sound of their movements. When she heard scratching, she aimed the light toward the sound. There, sitting in the darkness, were the Siamese. Their eyes glowed red in the beam of the flashlight.

"Scout. Abra. Stay there. Don't move."

When Katherine moved off the last stair, she stepped down into several inches of water. "Oh, geez, Colleen. The basement is flooded."

Colleen called, "Water? What? Can you see anything?"

"I see the cats. I'll get them and bring them over to you. You can help me take them outside and put them in their carrier."

"Okay, coming down."

The Siamese stood tall on top of a concrete block in front of a padded door. Scout jiggled the padlock while Abra stretched up on her hind legs, and toyed with something next to the door. She looked at Katherine, squeezed her eyes and cried a sad, "Raw."

Katherine reached over and found Abra's prize—a small key hanging on a hook.

"Mir-waugh," Scout cried, which sounded like "hurry up."

Colleen waded over to Katherine. "What is it?"

"A padlock key." Katherine inserted the key in the lock and the shackle opened. "Can you move that concrete block over? Push it with your foot."

Colleen moved over to do so, but stopped. "What about the cats? Shouldn't we get them to your vehicle, then come back?"

"Na-waugh," Scout bellowed.

The cats lunged off the concrete block, splashed to the bottom step and hopped up.

When the block was out of the way, Katherine opened the door. A low wattage lightbulb, dangling from a wire mounted in the ceiling, hardly illuminated the room. The walls were heavily padded like the door. Close to the entrance was a rolled-up carpet, soaking wet. When she stepped over it, something inside the carpet moaned. Falling to her knees, she unrolled a section and found Mum.

"Oh, I thought I'd died in me bed," Mum said weakly, then "Get me out of here. There's a maniac trying to kill me."

The Siamese dashed off the step and into the room. They trotted in front of Maggie Murphy and launched into a series of emphatic cries, all the while looking at the open door.

"What's wrong?" Katherine asked the cats, turning to see what they were frightened of. A tall shadow fell across the room. A well-built man in his forties grabbed Colleen by her hair and began choking her.

Colleen was kicking and fighting for her life.

Scout and Abra ran out of the room and leapt onto the man's back. Abra dug her claws into the man's head. Scout bit the man on the back of his neck. In a blur of frenzied felines, the man was so scratched he let go of Colleen and brought his hands up to defend himself. The cats sprung away from the assailant and trotted back to Mum's side.

Katherine pulled out her Glock and racked the slide to put the first bullet in the chamber. She aimed the gun at the man. "Get down on your knees and put your hands behind your back," she ordered.

Scout wildly sniffed the air with her fangs bared. She began to wail in a shrill, mournful cry.

"Okay. Okay. Only if you call off those cats!" he said.

Scout and Abra moved to the edge of the room and began grooming themselves. Abra paid special attention to the cut on one of her front paw pads.

The man fell to his knees and put his hands behind his back.

Colleen frantically punched in 911 and asked for emergency assistance at the Melody Manor. "My mother, Maggie Murphy, is in serious condition. She's very weak and hasn't eaten in several days. I need an ambulance and the police. That's right. Melody Manor on Main Street. We're in the basement. Come to the side entrance on the west side of the house," she said. The 911 operator began to ask other questions, but Colleen hung up. She then called the police. When Officer Grant answered, Colleen blurted, "This is Colleen Cokenberger. We found my mother in the basement of Melody Manor. I've called 911 and requested an ambulance and the police. Please get Chief Merrill over here ASAP."

Carrying a heavy-duty flashlight, Mrs. Richards slowly came down the stairs. "I know you girls are down here. You're trespassing. I'm calling the police." When she realized Katherine was pointing a gun at a man kneeling on the floor, she yelled, "Put that gun down. What are you doing to my son?"

Colleen, rubbing her neck, said, "Your son just tried to strangle me. And, the psycho kidnapped my mother."

"You're crazy. My son would never do such a thing. Put the gun down or I swear I'll hit you with my flashlight."

Katherine demanded, "Drop it! Move over next to your son and no one will get hurt."

Mrs. Richards reluctantly dropped the flashlight and waded over to her son. She said, "John, what a mess. I hope you turned off the water supply valve."

"Yes, I did, but what about me?"

"I'm sorry, honey, are you okay? Why is there a big bruise on your forehead?"

"I'm having a bad day."

Mum moaned, "Oh, for the love of Mary, get me out of here. They're both daft!"

Colleen comforted her, "Help is on its way."

Mum said in a weak voice, "That man lured me out here, then made me give him money. When I told him I wasn't giving him anymore, he came in my room in the middle of the night, put this cloth over my face, and I passed out. When I woke up, I was in this horrible room. I was so cold and hungry, I found an old rug and rolled myself up in it. Then I prayed."

"We're here, now."

Mum continued, "He threw in a bucket for me to go to the bathroom in. He never came back to check on me. I'm starving."

"Have you been drinking water?" Colleen asked, noticing the water seeping into the room from an opening underneath the door.

"Yes, I've been drinking that filthy water. I need a hospital."

"Yes, Mum, we'll get you there as soon as we can," Colleen explained, then pointed at the man kneeling on the floor outside the room. "Is that John Smith?"

"Yes," she spat. "And I'll hate him for what he's done to me 'til the day I die. He stole my money and my jewelry. He snatched my claddagh ring right off my finger."

"Mum, Katz has it. I'll explain later."

Katherine called inside to Colleen, "Are you okay? Did he hurt your neck?"

"Nothing to worry about."

Still aiming her Glock at John and his mother, and keeping a diligent eye on them, Katherine said to Mum, "I'm so relieved we found you. You're going to be okay, but I need Colleen for a few minutes." Then, she said to her friend, "Please get Scout and Abra out of here. Can you wrangle the both of them and get them to the carrier? Take them to the Outback. I left it unlocked. Power down a window a few inches so they don't overheat. The keys are under the right passenger floor mat."

"No, Katz, I can't leave Mum."

Mum said, "Save them, my love, like they saved me. Go quickly."

Colleen hesitated.

"If we wait any longer, the police sirens will totally freak the cats out," Katherine pleaded. "They'll bolt and we might never find them."

"But I can't leave you. What if one of them tries to get away?"

"Then I'll shoot them. Go, please."

Colleen reached down and easily picked up Abra, but Scout objected. "Stop, little lass. I have to get you two to safety." Scout reached up to be held. Picking her up,

Colleen cooed to the pair, "My good girls," then "Eww, you're wet. I'll find something to dry you off."

John Smith threatened, "I should have killed those cats from day one. They got out. Wrecked rooms. Tore up the plumbing. Now the damn basement is flooded. Mom, look what they did to me? I'm bleeding."

"My poor baby. We have to get you help. Dear, what were you doing down here? I thought you took your lady friend back to the airport."

The son didn't answer.

Katherine said to Mrs. Richards, "Then you knew Maggie Murphy was here and you lied to us about it?"

"I never said such a thing."

"Shut up, Mom. Don't say another word," John advised.

The loud sound of police sirens and an ambulance filled the air and startled the Siamese. Colleen clutched them tighter and hurried outside with two wet cats struggling to be put down. Colleen gently placed them in their carrier and got them to safety inside Katherine's vehicle.

Chief Merrill, pulled up in her cruiser with its emergency lights whirling and the sirens blaring. She parked behind John Smith's beat-up pickup. Officer Grant parked behind the chief. They both got out and approached Colleen. "What's going on?"

Colleen answered, in a quivering voice, "My mother is in the basement in terrible shape. John Smith kidnapped her and held her captive in the basement since their date Saturday night. He's down there now with Mrs. Richards."

The chief and Officer Grant took off running.

Colleen yelled after them, "Katz has a Glock pointed at them. She's licensed to carry a handgun."

The chief shouted back, "Stay where you are and direct the paramedics when they get here."

The chief and Officer Grant disappeared down the basement steps. "Police," Chief Merrill said in a loud voice.

Both officers had their guns drawn. The chief said to Katherine, "Stand down. Point your weapon down, remove the magazine and holster it."

Katherine did so and tucked the gun back in her jeans.

The chief aimed her gun at John. "John Smith, you are under arrest for criminal confinement, aggravated battery, and a cocktail of other charges I'm sure the prosecutor will mix up."

John groaned. "You again?"

The chief understood his reference. "Yes, me again. And, let's not forget you've violated your parole."

"What about those damn cats? Aren't you going to do something about them? They attacked me. What if they have rabies?"

"Well, John, it would be hard for me to do anything about cats, since I don't see any down here."

Katherine thought, *Give me your prison address and I'll mail you a copy of their rabies certificates.*

The chief turned to John's mother. "Sarah Smith Richards, you are charged with aiding and abetting a criminal."

"You can't do that," she protested. "I have a B&B to operate."

"That might be hard to do from jail."

Mrs. Richards complained, "I had no idea there was a woman in the basement. I never come down here. How would I have known?"

"Save it for your attorney," the chief said, then turned to Officer Grant, "Rudy, read Sarah her rights as you walk her to your vehicle. Put her in a holding cell."

"Yes, Chief."

"And, you Mr. Smith, stay on your knees and turn around to face the wall." John did as he was told. The chief handcuffed him and read him his rights, then handed him over to a third officer who had just shown up.

Two Melody paramedics came down the stairs and headed to the padded room. While one checked Maggie's vitals, the other began prepping her arm for an IV.

Colleen joined her mother. "Everything is going to be okay."

"T'was a nightmare to behold," Mum said. "I'm so happy to see you. I love you to the moon."

Colleen's voice choked, "I love you, too."

One of the paramedics said to Colleen, "Miss, can you move aside for a moment? We need to get your mother out of this rug and into a heated blanket."

"Yes, sir."

Once Mum was unrolled and placed in the blanket, she spoke to the paramedics, "I wouldn't be alive if it wasn't for Katz's cats."

The chief's ears perked up in interest.

"Oh, is that so, but ma'am, you need to be quiet," the paramedic said kindly.

Mum continued, "The Siamese visited me several times. They talked to me outside the door and I swear they even brought me water."

Colleen countered, "Mum, I don't think you'd be able to hear them. This seems to be a soundproof room."

"But I did. I did hear them."

The chief said to Katherine, "Interesting. Is this true?"

"It's possible."

"Where are the cats now?"

"Colleen put them in my vehicle."

"The Subaru Outback parked in the back?"

"Yes."

"Are you planning on leaving?"

"As soon as I can."

"I take it you have a license to carry a handgun?"

"Yes, I do. It's in my purse."

"Can I see it?"

"It's in the SUV."

"I'll also need to see your cats' rabies tags?"

"Yes, they're in my purse, too."

"What about the claddagh ring you called me about? Do you have it with you?" the chief asked.

"Yes, it's in my pocket."

The chief reached inside her jacket and removed an evidence bag. She opened it, and Katherine dropped the ring into it.

"Thank you, ma'am," she said, then advised, "I'll need your statement. I want to know every detail of how you found Maggie Murphy in the basement. And, I want a full account of what your cats were doing when you found her."

"Where do I go to give my statement?"

"Downtown to the station."

"Yes, I'll go, but I have a problem."

"What's that?"

"I need to tend to my cats. I think one of them hurt her paw."

The chief nodded. "Okay, I understand completely. I have a cat. I'm happy you're a good pet owner. Now, while you're giving your statement, your cats can be in the same room, mind you that they're in a cat carrier."

"Yes, thank you so much. I didn't want to leave them in my vehicle."

"And let one of the officers make a copy of your driver's license and your license to carry. And, proof your cats have been vaccinated."

"Will do."

"I trust you'll do these things because Chief London gave me a glowing report about you when I spoke to him."

"Thank you. He's a dear friend of mine."

The paramedics carried Mum up the basement steps and placed her on a gurney they'd left outside.

Standing at the foot of the stairs, Colleen said, "Katz, I'm riding with Mum to the hospital. Are you coming?"

"I want to, but the cats —"

"I understand. You don't have to come. Take the Siamese home. I called Daryl and he's on his way."

"Are you sure? I can call Jake to come and get them."

"No, I insist. You've done enough for us. I'll keep you posted," Colleen said, rushing off to join up with her mother and the paramedics.

The chief said, "My officers will be doing a thorough search of this house. We need to make sure there isn't any other woman being held captive."

"I pray there isn't."

"This means you have to leave the house now. You can't come back."

"Oh, I won't . . . ever!"

The chief turned and trudged up the basement stairs. Katherine followed her and stopped when she heard people speaking outside. The local press had arrived, and reporters were asking the chief a barrage of questions. She hoped none of them would try to interview her. She made it out the door and ten feet down the sidewalk when a young reporter approached. "Ma'am, do you know anything about this case?"

She deflected the question. "I was going to ask you the same thing."

The reporter quickly turned his attention to the growing throng of people who'd showed up, wanting to see what was going on.

Once in the SUV, Katherine checked on the cats and was surprised to find them sleeping, snuggled in the clean towel Colleen had placed in their cage. "I'm sorry, my treasures, to wake you up, but I need to check Abra's paw," she said, opening the gate.

"Na-waugh," Scout answered.

"Not your paw. Abra's."

Abra cried, "Raw," and pulled out her paw from underneath the towel.

"Good girl." Katherine examined the wound and was thankful it was no longer bleeding. "We'll have Dr. Sonny look at it first thing tomorrow morning," then to Scout, "I lied. I need to see your claws."

Scout refused to move her paws out from the warm towel.

"Maybe I should check your teeth to make sure none of them are broken."

"Na-waugh," Scout replied, more irritated.

"Okay, but I'll check later to make sure you didn't break a few biting that awful man's neck."

The Siamese muttered something to each other.

"Whatever that meant," Katherine said, closing the gate. "Let's get this show on the road. I have one more stop to make before we go home, then it will be a few hours before you can rejoin the other cats."

"Ma-waugh," Scout agreed sleepily.

Chapter Seventeen

Thursday

Stevie's Cabin

On the previous evening, when Stevie and Rachael arrived at the isolated cabin outside of Erie, they were both exhausted and quickly fell asleep snuggled on the sofa. Later, Stevie carried Rachael to the guest room and tucked her in, then went to his own room and fell back to sleep.

In the morning, Rachael woke up with something draped across her neck. It was warm, furry, and purred. "Intruder," she said happily. "My sweet girl." The ebony black kitten swiveled her large, pointed ears, squeezed her almond-shaped gold eyes, then mewed a sweet hello. "How did you get in here?" she asked, petting her.

Stevie knocked on the door, "Are you up?"

"Yes, come in."

Stevie opened the door. "How's my favorite girls?"

Rachael smiled. "How did Intruder get here? I thought she was at your other house."

"I woke up bright and early, drove over there and picked her up. I wrote a note to the cat sitter that I'll return

Intruder on Saturday before we leave to go back to Melody."

"It was very sweet of you to get her. I really wanted to see her. She's precious as ever."

"And, probably hungry. Let's say I rustle up breakfast. This ole boy is starving."

Rachael said, "I need to shower, but I have a wardrobe problem. Either I wear the clothes I had on yesterday for the next three days or—"

Stevie finished, "I went over to the storefront and packed up some of your clothes. Are jeans and T-shirts okay?"

"Perfect. Thanks so much for doing that."

"You shower and I'll make us breakfast."

"And coffee."

Intruder jumped off the bed and ran over to Stevie. She leaped up and landed on Stevie's thigh. "Ouch," he said, unhooking ten claws. He turned her over on her back and held her like a baby. "Your claws are like needles, little girl," then to Rachael, "We'll be in the kitchen."

Later, after breakfast, Stevie gave Rachael the grand tour of the cabin in the daylight. She fell in love with every room, but her favorite was the family room with its rough-hewn log walls and a rustic stone fireplace. A large picture window overlooked a heavily wooded area with trees displaying their autumn colors in gold, orange and red.

After their tour of the inside, they walked outside onto a wrap-around porch with four oak rocking chairs with cane seats.

Stevie said, "Sometimes in the early morning or just before it gets dark, I see deer walk out of the woods and eat the corn I put out for them."

"That's wonderful. I've always been a city girl and have missed out on that."

"Well, would my city girl like to take a drive?" Stevie asked, pulling Rachael into a hug.

"Sounds good to me. I'm ready any time."

"How about now?"

"Sure, but I need to call my grandmother's estate attorney."

"Okay. I'll be back in a minute. I have to go upstairs and get something," Stevie said, darting off.

Rachael sat down on one of the rocking chairs and pulled out of her pocket a burner phone she'd bought the night before. She also took out a piece of paper that had the attorney's phone number on it. The call went to voicemail, so she explained that on the previous morning, she'd faxed the affidavit to the bank. And sent a second fax to the attorney with her new mailing address. She was calling to verify that he'd received the fax and ask if he would text her if he hadn't. Just in case, she once again gave him the storefront address in Erie and also her new cellphone number. She disconnected the call and thought, *I don't think it's relevant to inform him I sent a third fax to my handler at the Witness Protection Program. I'm pretty much sure he doesn't know the address he's been using to correspond with me is affiliated with that program. That's okay by me. The fewer who know it, the better.*

While she waited for Stevie, she heard a rustling in a nearby pile of leaves. Two squirrels chased each other and ran up a tree. She laughed.

Stevie came back. "What's so funny?"

"I was watching the squirrels," she said, amused.

"Well, what you waitin' for? Git in the truck."

"Git," she mimicked.

"Yep, git." Stevie chuckled.

"Who taught you how to speak?" Rachael asked with an exaggerated nasal New York accent.

"My mama taught me down there in them hills and hollers of Kentucky."

Rachael burst out laughing. She climbed onto the passenger seat while Stevie got in behind the wheel.

He put the truck in gear and drove down a long, winding gravel driveway. Just before he came to a paved country road, he picked up a remote lying on the center console and clicked a button to open the chain-link security gate.

Rachael was impressed. "Is your entire property fenced? I couldn't tell last night."

"Yes, ma'am. Cost a fortune, but I wouldn't have it any other way."

"I'm happy you're private like I am."

He smiled and drove out onto the road, clicking the remote and closing the gate behind him.

"Where are we going?"

"Someplace you'll like," he said mysteriously.

"And where's that?"

"My wind turbine farm across from Chester's."

"Really?"

"I wouldn't kid you. Got the lawn chairs in the back."

"Is Chester's open?"

"Yep, but I'm sorry to say, he's not selling his famous BBQ."

"Why not?"

"It's a seasonal thing."

"What does he sell now?"

"Spiced apple cider, hot or cold, and the most mouthwatering pumpkin bread you've ever tasted."

"Oh, my goodness. We have to stop there on the way home."

"Thought you'd like to do that."

They rode in silence for a short time, then Rachael asked, "I have to ask you something and I want you to be totally honest. Has there been anyone since me?"

Stevie jammed on the brakes and pulled over. "Come closer."

She leaned in.

He grabbed the back of her neck and drew her close. He kissed her hard. "What do you think?"

"I guess that's a no."

"Damn, right," he said. "There isn't any other woman in this world that I want but you."

"That makes me happy."

"Don't get me wrong," Stevie said, starting back up again. "I ain't, I mean, I'm not a boy scout. But, after I met you, I made up my mind I never wanted to be involved with another woman for the rest of my life. What about you? Has there been anyone?"

"I haven't dated. There are guys who asked me out, but I always said no."

"That's good to know."

Stevie found the entrance to his wind turbine farm and turned in. He drove to the same exact location they'd had their first date on. He parked and got out.

Before Rachael could open her door, he opened it and gently pulled her out, stopping to kiss her another time.

Rachael hugged him and pulled away. "I really like it here. The air seems different now."

"It's cooling down. No more night vampires, so we don't have to douse ourselves with bug spray. Look over there," he pointed to the east side of his farm. "See the wooded area?"

"It's gorgeous with the trees turning colors."

"I own that land. It's been in my family for over a century. Locals call it the Sanders' homestead. I have a picture of my great-grandfather sitting on the porch."

"Cool, but where's the house?"

"Oh, it's gone now. It was an old dilapidated farmhouse. I had to tear it down. My brother, Dave, inherited the house and the land from my father's estate. Dave had many plans on what he was going to do with it, but they didn't pan out."

"What kind of plans?"

"Dave wanted to have a house built for his wife and family, but she didn't want to move from their house in Erie, so he put the land up for sale—"

"And you bought it," Rachael finished.

"Yes, ma'am." Stevie's blue eyes shone brightly in the sun.

"I'm confused. You said a while ago that you were from Kentucky."

"My mother was from Kentucky. When she married my father, he brought her to Erie. When they divorced, she moved back."

"So, I take it, your great-grandfather Sanders farmed the land over there."

Stevie laughed. "Sort of. He grew enough corn to make his special brew."

"Special brew?"

"Yep, moonshine. During the Prohibition he made a lot of money in the bootlegging business."

"Oh, okay," she said, amused.

"Someday we'll go for a hike in the woods and I'll show you the old still."

"Fun." She smiled, then asked, "Is your cabin on that land?"

"No, that's a separate parcel by itself. I'm in the process of buying the parcel that's next to it."

"Really? I'm impressed. Is it wooded?"

"No, it's farmland, not a tree on it. When the sale is final, I'll rent the land to the same energy-conglomerate I'm working with now."

"How many turbines will be put up?"

"I'm figuring at least twenty. Maybe more. We'll see."

"Seems like there's a lot going on in your life since I saw you last. Call me nosy, but what about your electric contracting business?"

"With the new turbines, my goal is to give up that business and work at home."

"Work at home? Doing what?"

"It sort of depends on you. Now, enough of my talking about my family history and business ventures. I brought you here to ask you something."

"What?" she asked curiously.

Stevie took her by the hand and led her to the concrete pad of the closet turbine. "Stand right there and don't move," he said, heading back to the truck and getting something from the center console.

When he returned, he got down on one knee and said, "Rachael Thomas, will you marry me?" His handsome face searched hers for an answer.

Rachael's eyes brimmed with tears. "Oh, Stevie," she said.

"Will you start a new life with me?"

"Yes," she said. "It will be a perfect life."

"And live with me in the cabin?"

"Oh, yes. It's my dream."

Stevie rose and took her in his arms. He kissed her tenderly, then stood back and took a black velvet ring box out of his pocket. He flipped it open and showed it to her. Inside was a one-carat diamond set in platinum. It glistened in the sun.

Rachael praised, "Oh, my, it's beautiful."

Stevie took her left hand and placed the ring on her finger.

"It fits," she exclaimed.

"I knew it would," he said confidently, pulling her into another embrace.

Chapter Eighteen

One Week Later

Leaving Melody

Rachael drove her used Mazda onto the gravel driveway of her friend Ashley's house on the outskirts of Melody. She couldn't stop smiling as she thought about how her life had changed in just a few days. She'd regained her legal name and inherited her grandmother's money. She was officially free from the Witness Protection Program to do whatever she liked. She'd reunited with Stevie and looked forward to a future with him. She was genuinely happy for the first time in a long while.

She parked, got out, and walked inside the fenced area in front of the house. In the yard were several stray cats that Ashley took care of. She reached down to pet them. "Hi, kids," she said. "Is your mommy home?"

Ashley opened her door and said, animated, "Girl, I'm so glad you came to say goodbye to me. I'm going to miss you."

"I'm going to miss you, too."

As Rachael walked in, a streak of sleek black fur darted out from under the sofa and made a direct beeline for her. Rachael reached down to pick her up. "Shadow, my precious darling. You get prettier every day."

The cat began to purr loudly.

Rachael kissed her on top of her head. "Sweet girl."

"Are you all moved out of your apartment?" Ashley asked.

"Stevie just finished loading up my stuff in his truck. He had to get gas, which explains why he's not with me right now. I'm supposed to meet up with him at the apartment's parking lot."

"I'm hoping someday I'll get to meet him. I mean I talked to him at the roadhouse, but that's different. Someday I want you to bring him over and I'll fix a fancy Italian meal for the two of you."

"Yes, someday we will."

"Promise?"

"I promise."

"Oh, then, you don't want to keep him waiting."

"I want to thank you for being my friend. Here's a going-away present that I don't want you to say no to. Promise?"

"Depends on what it is."

"Well, then I can't give it to you," Rachael teased.

"Oh, shucks, give it to me." Ashley laughed loudly.

Rachael handed her a small envelope and watched in delight as her friend opened it.

Ashley said happily, "A gift card for a hundred bucks," then frowned, "Oh, this is way too much. I can't accept this."

"It's not for you."

"Well, then who's it for?"

"Your cats."

"You are so precious to think of them." Ashley smiled. "Thank you so much."

"Once a month I'll reload additional money, so you'll never be strapped for cash again to feed your cats."

"Oh, you are too kind. Every time I feed them, I'll say, 'This is from my friend, Sally.'"

Rachael didn't correct her. She hadn't told Ashley what her legal name was. She'd do that some other time.

"So, when's the big wedding?"

"We're not having a big wedding. In fact, we're getting married by a justice of the peace."

"Where? When?"

"We don't know yet." Rachael wanted to say that the ceremony would be held at the cabin with very few guests, just family and a few friends. And, since Rachael's family were deceased, it would mostly consist of a few members of Stevie's family, and especially Salina. She hoped Salina would attend, but didn't know what kind of reception she'd get when Stevie and she told her the news.

"I'm so glad the two of you hooked up again."

Rachael beamed. "He truly is the love of my life and I plan on holding onto him forever."

"Just like in one of those Hallmark movies." Ashley grinned.

"I have to leave now. We'll chat later. I'll text you in a few days."

"But wait. I have a present for you."

"You don't have to give me a present."

"Oh, yes, I do. Wait just a second." Ashley ran off to her bedroom, then returned holding a brand-new cat carrier with the sales tag still attached.

"What's this for?"

"For Shadow to ride in style."

"Shadow?"

"Ah, duh, the one snuggled in your arms."

Big tears formed in Rachael's eyes.

"No need to cry. From the first time I saw you with Shadow, I knew there was something special between you. I want to give you Shadow as your wedding present."

"But won't you miss her?"

"Of course, I will, but she's bonded to you. And, look at it this way, with Shadow gone, I'll have room for one more cat who needs my special attention."

"You're truly wonderful."

"Raw-owl," Shadow agreed.

Rachael said, "That's the first time I've heard her meow."

"She's basically a very quiet cat, but when she wants something that's a different story. She can be very vocal."

"I'm glad you took her in."

"Me, too," Ashley agreed. She put the cat carrier on top of her dining room table, opened the gate, and placed a folded towel inside.

Rachael moved over and put Shadow in. The cat settled down and began making biscuits on the towel.

Ashley closed the gate. "I'll help you carry her to your car."

"Thanks, but I can manage. I'll talk to you soon," Rachael said, hugging her.

"Drive safely," Ashley said, standing in the doorway.

"I will. Take care of yourself."

Ashley laughed. "I always do and if I can't, I'll bust out my persuader."

Rachael grinned, walked to her car, and placed the carrier on the front passenger seat. She tugged the seat belt over it to stabilize it in case Shadow liked to rock the cage.

Once on the highway to meet up with Stevie, Rachael said to the cat, "In a few minutes, I have someone for you to meet. He's tall, handsome, and loves cats. When we get to our new home, I have someone else for you to meet. Her name is Intruder and she's black just like you. She's much younger though. She's a kitten, so I hope you can take her under your wing and teach her what she needs to know."

"Raw-owl," Shadow approved.

"Oh, and by the way, you're the best gift ever."

Chapter Nineteen

Two Weeks Later

At the Pink Mansion

Katherine and Jake invited Colleen and Daryl over for dinner. She closed the pocket doors to the formal dining room to prevent the cats from coming into the room. She chose a burgundy damask tablecloth to cover the antique table and a floral arrangement of pink roses and white carnations as a centerpiece. She set the table with her great aunt's Haviland dishes and silver flatware. Jake placed a water glass and wine goblet next to each plate.

When Colleen and Daryl arrived, Katherine seated them, while Jake poured each a glass of Cabernet, then he served a thick slice of beef prime rib accompanied by a tangy horseradish sauce.

Daryl admired, "I can't get over how terrific this room is, from the rose-colored chandelier to the Victorian wallpaper. A photograph of this room belongs in a magazine."

Katherine smiled. "Thank you, Daryl."

Then Daryl said to Jake, "This looks really good."

"It's Jake's specialty," Katherine said facetiously.

"More like it's takeout from the Erie Hotel," Colleen said in a playful voice.

"Hey, I heard that, but I made the sides," Jake defended.

"I made the salad," Katherine added.

"So, Katz, where are the cats? Shouldn't they be pounding the pocket doors to get in?" Colleen asked.

Katherine giggled. "Jake used his secret weapon."

"What's that?" Daryl asked.

Jake sat down and smiled. "Pan-seared tuna steaks. They love it. They're in the kitchen feasting on the best ahi tuna steaks money can buy. I'm sure they're in cat heaven."

After they savored every tidbit of their food and cleared their plates, Colleen said, "Mum texted and said she received a letter from Melody's prosecutor. It seems she'll have to relive her nightmare and testify against John Smith."

"I got the same letter, didn't you?" Katherine asked.

"No, should I?"

Daryl said, "I'm sure you'll be getting one soon."

"When the case goes to trial, and we need to testify, I vote the three of us book rooms at a hotel in Scottsburg and drive to Melody," Katherine said.

"Why, Katz, does this mean you don't want to stay at Melody Manor?" Colleen kidded.

"Never again," Katherine added.

"How's Maggie doing though? Is she okay?" Jake asked.

"She gets stronger every day. She said the hardest part of the ordeal was not knowing if she'd live to see us again," Colleen said, tearing up.

"We're so thankful she's alive," Katherine said.

"She still insists that Scout and Abra saved her life, that they brought her water, and talked to her through the door."

Katherine laughed. "I can just hear them muttering their Siamese language. But, I'm not too sure they brought her water. I mean, do you think the cats deliberately damaged the pipes to cause a flood that would seep into Mum's room?"

"Of course, they did." Colleen grinned.

"Okay, so if they did, let's keep it our little secret. I don't want the news media folks getting ahold of this."

"Lips are sealed," Daryl said, pretending to zip his lips.

Colleen snickered. "When it comes to Katz's and Jake's cats and what they do, my lips have been zipped for a long time."

"I wonder what kind of sentence John Smith will get?" Katherine asked.

"Since he's an ex-con, the judge will take that into consideration," Daryl answered. "I'd say twenty years or more."

"What about his mother?" Colleen asked.

"I hope she loses her bed and breakfast license and never rents out rooms in her house again," Jake said bitterly.

"I can never forgive her for not telling us that Mum stayed at the B&B. She knew it and blatantly lied to us," Katherine added. "When she went out-of-town that weekend and came back Monday morning, she should have asked her son if he'd taken Mum back to the airport, yet she didn't."

"Sweet Pea, we don't know that as a fact," Jake said. "Maybe she did ask him and he gave her some bogus answer."

"If she'd only told the truth in the first place, Katz and I could have gone to the police on that Monday and demanded that they search the place," Colleen lamented. "Because of her negligence, she caused Mum to have two more days in hell."

Jake tried to steer the conversation away from the nightmare at Melody Manor. "Oh, maybe we should talk about something else."

Katherine wasn't finished yet. "I think Mrs. Richards should be charged with criminal intent to hit me with a heavy flashlight."

"She was more concerned about throwing her flashlight in the water than you aiming a gun at her," Colleen said.

"Plus, she didn't ask her son if he was okay until she'd found out if the water supply valve had been shut off. I mean, the guy had a giant hematoma on his forehead."

"Maybe the house meant more to her than her son," Jake said.

"She was daft in more ways than one," Colleen commented.

"She was very eccentric and had a thing against lightbulbs," Katherine said, tongue in cheek.

Colleen tipped her head back and laughed.

Daryl said, smiling, "I don't think wielding a flashlight to cause bodily harm is in the criminal code, but I could be wrong."

"Stevie is testifying," Katherine said.

Colleen said, shocked, "You talked to Stevie? I thought you weren't speaking to him because he failed to warn us about John Smith—"

"I'm kind of changing my opinion about that."

"How?"

"I think Stevie had a hunch, but couldn't prove it."

"But, Katz, why was he in Melody? The same place where Mum went missing? The same time we were there looking for her?"

"He had a valid reason. I'm not at liberty to talk about it now," Katherine said in a light-hearted tone, which begged for someone to ask her for more information.

"Oh, it's official police business? You sound like Chief Merrill," Colleen said.

Jake laughed. "Oh, come on, Katz, spill the beans to Colleen and Daryl. Everyone at the Red House diner has been talking about it for days."

Daryl whined, "That's not fair. I never go to that diner. What gives? Katz, spit it out!"

"The day after Colleen and I checked into the Melody Manor, Stevie drove to Melody to find Rachael."

"What?" Colleen said incredulously. "Why did he think she was in Melody? I thought the Feds would move her to Montana or some other sparsely populated area."

"Stevie knew John Smith. They worked together in the electrical shop at the prison in Michigan City."

Colleen gave an "uh-huh, I told you so" glance directed at Katherine.

"John contacted Stevie on Facebook. They started emailing each other. Stevie sent John a picture of his beloved—"

"Rachael," Colleen finished.

"John called Stevie and said he'd found her working at a popular Melody restaurant."

"No way. Really?" Colleen asked.

"That's how Stevie ended up in Melody. He was looking for Rachael. He didn't text us because he didn't want anything to mess up his hooking up with her again."

"Makes sense," Jake said. "I'd do the same thing."

Katherine reached over and squeezed his hand.

Colleen asked, "Did he find her?"

"Yes, at Rusty's Roadhouse where she's a server. She'd just started her shift and asked him to meet her after work at five p.m. On the way out of the restaurant, Stevie ran into John, who asked him to go to breakfast at the Melody Café. Stevie had lots of time to kill so he said yes. When he pulled in front of the café, he saw the missing person flyer on a pole next to where he parked. He became suspicious of John when he made a derogatory comment about the woman on the flyer.

"What did he say?" Colleen asked, with her face clouding up in anger.

"Something about the woman in the picture was some old hag wanting attention and wasn't actually missing at all. It sent off a red flag to Stevie. Then, after the chief came into the café and talked to the two of them, Stevie had an intuitive feeling that John knew something about Mum."

"At that point, why didn't he tell the chief?"

"Because he knew if he told her, she'd have him come down to the station and sign a witness statement. That would take time, and Stevie didn't want anything to interfere with his meeting Rachael later when she finished her shift."

"I can see his point, my sweet Colleen," Daryl said. "If it was me in that same situation, I'd wait until I had you back in my arms again before I notified the chief."

"You're adorable," Colleen said, looking at her new husband adoringly. "But isn't that obstructing justice?"

"Sounds like Stevie didn't have anything definitive," Jake said. "Just because someone calls someone else an old hag doesn't mean that they caused "said hag" bodily harm."

"Okay, let me finish," Katherine said. "It was during this breakfast that Stevie realized that John could be abusive to women. He suspected that John might have information regarding Mum, but he didn't have enough evidence to turn him into the police."

"Wait, if this is the case, why is Stevie testifying?"

"Because after he was escorted to the station by a Melody police officer, Stevie gave key information the chief needed to hear to confirm her own suspicions, and that was John met Mum on an online dating site—"

Jake finished, "And picked her up at the Louisville Airport and brought her to Melody. Am I right, Katz?"

"You nailed it. The flyer didn't say anything about an online dating site or mention the Louisville Airport, so

Stevie couldn't make the connection. The flyer said 'last seen in Melody.'"

Daryl asked, "Here's the key question? Did Stevie hook up with Rachael?"

Colleen said hurriedly, "You don't have to tell us, Katz, if Stevie asked you not to."

"But I didn't hear it from Stevie."

"Who'd you hear it from?"

"Salina. She knows everything. I haven't talked to Stevie. I haven't received a text from Stevie. I haven't seen him since we've been back."

Daryl said, "The suspense is killing me."

Katherine leaned back in her chair and said, "Yes, after Stevie was interviewed by the chief and signed his statement, Stevie and Rachael got back together. Stevie's in Melody at this very moment moving Rachael back to Erie."

Daryl said, confused, "What about the Witness Protection Program?"

"She opted out. She thinks the mob will never bother her again and that they've moved on to other fish in the sea."

"Katz, I don't think the word mob and fish go well together in a sentence. Remember that line in the *Godfather* where *Luca Brasi sleeps with the fishes*?" Colleen grinned.

"Okay, in other words, Rachael thinks the mob has forgotten her because she's a little fish in the sea. How's that, Carrot Top?" Katherine quipped.

Jake asked, "Where's she going to live?"

"This I don't know. Salina said her dad hadn't told her yet. She thought Rachael would move back into the downtown storefront she bought last summer."

"Oh, I get it. Stevie knows where she's moving, but didn't want to tell his blabber mouth daughter." Colleen covered her mouth and giggled. "Did I say that?"

Katherine defended. "I wouldn't quite call Salina a blabber mouth. I think both Stevie and Rachael are very private and we should respect her privacy."

"How's that going to happen when the whole town is talking about her right now?" Jake asked.

Katherine shook her head. "Don't know."

"I'm happy for Stevie. He's had some hard knocks in his life and I hope Rachael makes him happy," Colleen said.

"This is big news," Daryl said. "No wonder the diner crowd is going nuts, but what are they saying exactly? Surely everybody in town doesn't know that Rachael was part of the Witness Protection Program."

Jake answered, "No, they don't. The latest gossip is that last July, Rachael dumped Stevie, moved out of town, then changed her mind and begged Stevie to take her back."

"There has to be some people in town who know that Rachael went back East to testify against the mob. It was all over the national news," Katherine said, rolling her eyes.

"Apparently those folks don't eat at the diner," Jake kidded.

"I think Stevie will have a problem with his daughter not liking Rachael," Colleen noted.

"Salina said she's giving Rachael another chance," Katherine volunteered. "She wants her dad to be happy. But most of all, she wants to make amends with Rachael. She feels bad about not asking her first if it was okay to post a video that, as we all know, went viral and put a lot of people in danger."

"Not to mention the two police officers that were shot by the hitman," Daryl added.

Jake put in his two cents. "If the two of them can't agree, Salina will be out of the picture for a few years. She's moving away from home to start college this summer."

"Where's she going to school?" Colleen asked.

"She's been admitted to NYU. She wants to be a journalist," Katherine said.

"Wow, that's impressive," Daryl agreed.

Katherine beamed. "I'm proud of her."

Jake rose from his chair and said, "Save your fork. We've got pie."

"Coconut cream pie?" Colleen asked hopefully.

"Jake's specialty." Katherine winked.

"That's one thing Jake has over the Erie Hotel. His pie tastes better," Daryl complimented.

Jake opened the door to the kitchen and six felines darted in. "Oops, I didn't mean to release the Kraken."

Scout and Abra walked in with their tails intertwined; they leaped onto a side chair and sat tall in a regal pose. Lilac, Abby and Crowie raced in, jumped to the sideboard, to the top of the wood window valance and leaned over like vultures scanning the table for leftovers.

Daryl said, "Whoa, cats. That was a gold medal jump."

Dewey slowly strolled in, looking around the room for his buddy, Iris. "Mao! Mao!" the Siamese cried.

Katherine said knowingly, "Okay, we have a cat missing. I bet I know where she is." Katherine lifted up the tablecloth and peeked underneath the table. She found Iris sitting on top of Colleen's bag. "Miss Siam, what are you doing?"

"Yowl," the guilty cat cried, stretching, then trotted over to Dewey and began washing his ear.

Jake and Daryl belted out a loud laugh.

"Better check your purse for any missing items," Katherine suggested, smiling.

"Oh, I'm glad you mentioned my bag. Mum and I have a present to give to Scout and Abra."

The Siamese swiveled their ears in interest.

Colleen reached into her bag and drew out a small box. She opened it and took out two cat collars with charms attached to them. "They're the breakaway kind so if the lasses get tangled in something they can get loose."

"Oh, how sweet and they even have charms," Katherine observed.

"Yeah. The shamrock charm is for Scout because she brought us luck that day and the Claddagh is for Abra who led you to Mum's ring."

"Thank you so much." Katherine got up, took the collars and went over to the Siamese. She put the first one on Scout, then the second one on Abra. The Siamese sisters slowly blinked their blue eyes in delight.

Colleen grabbed her cell and took a pic of the Siamese. "I'm texting this to Mum right now."

The blissful moment lasted for a few seconds, then Scout bit Abra on the back of her neck and Abra returned the favor. They both launched off the chair and sped out of the room, followed by five other felines. The pounding of their paws made the old wood floors creak until they ran out of audible range.

"Swoosh," Daryl commented.

"The kraken-cats have left the room," Katherine said, laughing.

Dear Reader . . .

Thank you so much for reading my book. Over the past few years, I have completely enjoyed writing all twelve of the Cats that . . . Cozy Mystery books.

I love it when my readers write to me. I try to answer all emails within twenty-four hours.

Email me at: **karenannegolden@gmail.com**

For all of you, who will write positive reviews on Amazon and/or Goodreads, thank you so much. I very much appreciate it. Help others enjoy this book, too, by recommending it to family, friends, and book clubs.

I love to post pictures of my cats on my Facebook pages, and would enjoy learning about your pets as well. Follow me @ **https://www.facebook.com/karenannegolden**

Binge reading adds zero calories. If you are new to the series, the following pages describe my other books. If you love mysteries with cats, don't miss these action-packed page turners.

Thanks again.

Karen

The Cats that Surfed the Web

Book One in *The Cats that . . .* Cozy Mystery series

If you haven't read the first book, *The Cats that Surfed the Web*, you can download the Kindle or paperback version on Amazon.

The Cats that Surfed the Web, is an action-packed, exhilarating read. When Katherine "Katz" Kendall, a career woman with cats, discovers she's the sole heir of a huge inheritance, she can't believe her good luck. She's okay with the conditions in the will: Move from New York City to the small town of Erie, Indiana, live in her great aunt's pink Victorian mansion, and take care of an Abyssinian cat. With her three Siamese cats and best friend Colleen riding shotgun, Katz leaves Manhattan to find a former housekeeper dead in the basement. There are people in the town who are furious that they didn't get the money. But who would be greedy enough to get rid of the rightful heir to take the money and run?

Four adventurous felines help Katz solve the crimes by mysteriously "searching" the Internet for clues. If you love cats, especially cozy cat mysteries, you'll enjoy this series.

The Cats that Chased the Storm

Book Two in *The Cats that* . . . Cozy Mystery series

It's early May in Erie, Indiana, and the weather has turned most foul. We find Katherine "Katz" Kendall, heiress to the Colfax fortune, living in a pink mansion, caring for her three Siamese and Abby the Abyssinian. Severe thunderstorms frighten the cats, but Scout is better than any weather app. A different storm is brewing, however, with a discovery that connects great uncle William Colfax to the notorious gangster John Dillinger. Why is the Erie Historical Society so eager to get William's personal papers? Is the new man in Katherine's life a fortune hunter? Will Abra mysteriously reappear, and is Abby a magnet for danger?

A fast-paced whodunit, the second book in "The Cats that" series involves four extraordinary felines that help Katz unravel the mysteries in her life.

The Cats that Told a Fortune

Book Three in *The Cats that* . . . Cozy Mystery series

    In the land of corn mazes and covered bridge festivals, a serial killer is on the loose. Autumn in Erie, Indiana means cool days of intrigue and subterfuge. Katherine "Katz" Kendall settles into her late great aunt's Victorian mansion with her five cats. A Halloween party at the mansion turns out to be more than Katz planned for. Meanwhile, she's teaching her first computer training class, and a serial killer is murdering young women. Along the way, Katz and her cats uncover important clues to the identity of the killer, and find out about Erie's local crime family . . . the hard way.

The Cats that Played the Market

Book Four in *The Cats that* . . . Cozy Mystery series

A blizzard blows into Indiana, bringing gifts, gala events, and a ghastly murder to heiress Katherine "Katz" Kendall. It's Katherine's birthday, and she gets more than she bargains for when someone evil from her past comes back to haunt her. After all hell breaks loose at the Erie Museum's opening, Katherine and her five cats unwittingly stumble upon clues that help solve a mystery. But has Scout lost her special abilities? Or will Katz find that another one of her amazing felines is a super-sleuth?

With the cats providing clues, it's up to Katherine and her friends to piece together the murderous puzzle . . . before the town goes bust!

The Cats that Watched the Woods

Book Five in *The Cats that* . . . Cozy Mystery series

What have the extraordinary cats of millionaire Katherine "Katz" Kendall surfed up now? "Idyllic vacation cabin by a pond stocked with catfish." It's July in Erie, Indiana, and steamy weather fuels the tension between Katz and her fiancé, Jake. Katz rents the cabin for a private getaway, though Siamese cats, Scout and Abra, demand to go along. How does a peaceful, serene setting go south in such a hurry? Is the terrifying man in the woods real, or is he the legendary ghost of Peace Lake? It's up to Katz and her cats to piece together the mysterious puzzle. The fifth book in the popular "The Cats that . . . Cozy Mystery" series is a suspenseful, thrilling ride that will keep you on the edge of your seat.

The Cats that Stalked a Ghost

Book Six in *The Cats that . . .* Cozy Mystery series

While Katherine and Jake are tying the knot at her pink mansion, a teen ghost has other plans, which shake their Erie, Indiana town to its core. How does a beautiful September wedding end in mistaken identity . . . and murder? What does an abandoned insane asylum have to do with a spirit that is haunting Katz? Colleen, a paranormal investigator at night and student by day, shows Katz how to communicate with ghosts. An arsonist is torching historic properties. Will the mansion be his next target? Ex-con Stevie Sanders and the Siamese play their own stalking games, but for different reasons. It's up to Katz and her extraordinary felines to solve two mysteries: one hot, one cold. Seal-point Scout wants a new adventure fix, and littermate Abra fetches a major clue that puts an arsonist behind bars.

The Cats that Stole a Million

Book Seven in *The Cats that . . .* Cozy Mystery series

Millionaire Katherine, aka Katz, husband Jake and their seven cats return to the pink mansion after the explosion wreaked havoc several months earlier. Now the house has been restored, will it continue to be a murder magnet? Erie, Indiana is crime-free for the first time since heiress Katherine and her cats moved into town. Everyone is at peace until domestic harmony is disrupted by an uninvited visitor from Brooklyn. Why is Katz's friend being tracked by a NYC mob? Meanwhile, ex-con Stevie Sanders wants to go clean, but ties to dear old Dad (Erie's notorious crime boss) keep pulling him back. Murder, lies, and a million-dollar theft have Katz and her seven extraordinary cats working on borrowed time to unravel a mystery.

The Cats that Broke the Spell

Book Eight in *The Cats that . . .* Cozy Mystery series

When a beautiful professor is accused of being a witch, she retreats to her cabin in the woods. Soon a man dressed like a scarecrow begins to stalk her, and vandals leave pentagrams at her front gate. The town of Erie, Indiana has never known a witch hunt, but after the first accusation, the news spreads like wildfire. "She stole another woman's husband, then murdered him," people raged in the local diner. "She uses her black cats to cast spells to do her evil deeds!" But what do the accusers really want? How is Erie's crime boss involved? In the meantime, while the pink mansion's attic is being remodeled, Katz, Jake and their seven felines move out to a rural farmhouse, which is next door to the "witch." They find themselves drawn into a deadly conflict on several fronts. It's up to Katz and her seven extraordinary cats to unravel the tangle of lies before mass hysteria wrecks the town. Murder, mayhem, and a cold case make this book a thrilling, action-packed read that will keep you guessing until the very end.

The Cats that Stopped the Magic

Book Nine in *The Cats that . . .* Cozy Mystery series

This classic whodunit boasts a new cast of characters: a self-centered magician, a compulsive gambler, a sweet cat wrangler and her grandmother, a caring nurse, and a wealthy couple. How are their lives intertwined with a show cat named Abra? In 2009, two Siamese cats performed in Magic Harry's Hocus-Pocus show, in front of hundreds of devoted fans. But their lives were far from magical, and their careers were cut short when Abra was stolen backstage after a performance. Why did the magician increase the insurance on Abra days before she disappeared? Was Abra stolen and sold on the black market? Or did anonymous cat-lovers rescue her from a life-threatening situation? A wealthy tycoon wants a Siamese cat with a specific look for his dying wife. Why? Four years later, Abra ends up in an animal shelter. Where had she been during this time? Back in Erie, Indiana, Katherine and Jake work on borrowed time to piece the puzzle together before Magic Harry tries to take Abra away from them.

The Cats that Walked the Haunted Beach

Book Ten in *The Cats that* . . . Cozy Mystery series

This fast-paced mystery is chock-full of coincidences and bizarre twists. When Colleen and Daryl get together to plan their wedding, they can't agree on anything. Colleen is at her wits' end. Best friend Katherine votes for a time-out and proposes a girls' retreat to a town named Seagull, which borders Lake Michigan and the famous Indiana dunes. Mum is adamant they stay in a rented cabin right on the beach. Against Katz's better judgment, she agrees with Mum's plan — only on one condition: she's bringing Scout and Abra, who become very upset when she's away from them. With the Siamese in tow, Katherine and Colleen head to the dunes to find that Mum's weekend retreat is far from ideal. The first night, they have a paranormal experience and learn that a ghost walks the beach when someone is going to be murdered. Meanwhile, ex-con Stevie has a date with a woman he met online. But this news doesn't prevent the town gossips from spreading a rumor that he's having an affair with a married woman. How does Abra finding a wallet lead to a mix-up with dangerous consequences? It's up to Katz and her extraordinary cats to unravel a deadly plot that ends in murder.

The Cats that Cooked the Books

Book Eleven in *The Cats that* . . . Cozy Mystery series

Amazon bestselling all-star author does it again with her 11th book in "The Cats that . . .Cozy Mystery" series. It's steamy hot in Erie, Indiana. The town is crime-free until a hitman shows up. Katz, Jake and their seven cats are happy at the pink mansion until a blast from the past blows in, leaving dire results in its wake. How does a coincidental meeting trigger such disastrous consequences? Handsome Stevie has finally found the woman of his dreams, or has he? Why does a viral video bring disaster to the small town? Murder and havoc make this book a thrilling, suspenseful read that will keep you guessing to the very end. It's up to Katz and her extraordinary cats to solve the puzzle before more bullets fly.

Acknowledgements

I wish to thank my husband, Jeff, who edited the first draft of this book. Thanks for supporting my creative process and helping me clarify complicated plot points.

Thank you, Vicki for being my amazing editor. Over the years, I have been thrilled to work with you and am thankful we have taken this journey together. You've been my lucky charm.

Also, thanks Rob, my favorite book cover artist. I love your work. Your spin on the book cover set the mood. I particularly love this cover.

Thanks, Ramona and her dog Louie for beta reading my book. Mona has taken this journey with me since my third book, *The Cats that Told a Fortune*.

Thank you, Bob for your advice on ballistics.

Also, I wish to thank my friends, Sandy and Christy, who invited me to accompany them to a B&B in a lovely Victorian home, located in southern Indiana on the banks of the Ohio River. I was inspired by the experience to write this book.

Thanks to my loyal readers, my family, and friends.

The Cats that . . . Cozy Mystery series would never be without the antics of my furry friends. My husband and I have many cats, ranging in ages from five to eighteen-years-old. All of our cats were either rescues or gifts.

"Release the Kraken" is a line from the 2010 movie, *Clash of the Titans*.

Printed in Great Britain
by Amazon